MARK TOWSE

THE BUCKET LIST

THE BUCKET LIST
©2022 by Mark Towse and Chisto Healy

ISBN: 9798360721550

Cover, Layout, Interior
K. Trap Jones

www.theevilcookie.com

Dedication

Mark Towse:
To my mother, for always being my first reader and one hell of an editor. Love you, Mum. To my father for gracing me with one hell of a sense of humour. He's not doing too well right now, which breaks my heart. Love you, Dad.

Chisto Healy:
To Jon Soda James and Gloria—my longest and dearest friends and two people who have always understood that life should be lived to the fullest.

Marge and Alby

"**A**re all the rooms set up and ready, Albert?"

"Yes, dear."

"Did you put fresh towels out and make sure the rooms had loo roll?"

"Yes, dear."

"Vacuum all through?"

"Yes, dear."

"Fluff the pillows?"

"Uh-uh."

"Put a chocolate on each?"

Silence.

"Albert?"

He nods but turns his stare to the floor and slides his hands into his pockets. "Don't think anyone will come in this rain anyway."

"Come here, Alby."

The shortened version of his name usually carries three possible implications: nurturing, scolding, or sexy time. Pinching at the saggy skin of his nut bag through the pocket lining, he begins shuffling towards her. He gets tired so easily these days, and after the excitement of earlier, just wants to sit down and reminisce for a while—sexy time by himself while the memories are still fresh.

"Look at me, Alby."

Close enough to hear his wife's throaty rattle, Albert pauses, keeping his stare fixed on the gaudy pink slippers. He buries his hands further into his pockets, cupping his balls as if preparing to offer them as a gesture. Still, he can't prevent the smile tugging at the corners of his dry, chapped lips as he recalls the woman's wide eyes and mouth contorted to a silent scream.

"Eyes, Alby." Marge drags her thumb across his grinning mouth, forcing a wet smacking sound from his lips.

Squeezing at his testicles, Albert lifts his stare towards the plump finger she holds in front of him. It's blurred and out of focus, his eyes pointing in different directions and offering a watery resolution, but he sees the smear of brown. He releases his wrinkled face from the smile that held it taut, his mini-fantasy well and truly over.

"Alby?"

Margaret has two looks, one for him and one for the outsiders, but sometimes they merge, especially if her patience becomes stretched like it is now. "Well?" Another harsh rattle emerges from her throat.

"I ate them," he says softly.

"Pardon, Alby?"

He clears his throat, feeling pressure behind his eyes. "I ate them."

"One more time, Alby." Another crackle, another deep exhale. "Only I could have sworn you said you ate the last two chocolates when I explicitly gave you instructions not to."

"But they were the good ones with the mint in 'em." The sting is intense, accompanied by a flash of white light and a ringing in his ears that takes him back to another time. He straightens up and bites at his lip but can't prevent the release of a tear.

"Oh, Alby," Margaret says softly, bringing him into her bosom. "I'm so sorry, petal." She begins stroking his bald head, fingers roaming over liver spots like a child playing connect the dots, gently swaying left to right as she does. "I just want things to be right, my dear."

Albert watches his solitary tear run down his wife's sagging left breast until it disappears into oblivion. Over the thud of her heartbeat and the dampening ringing left by the strike of her knobby knuckles, he's just able to hear the gentle patter of rain. He turns his stare to the window, tracking the path of more water droplets as they carve their way down the panes. "Sorry, dear. I'll do better."

"It's okay, my love." Clamping his head between her big hands full of stubby fingers and enough palm hair to earn her a spot as a werewolf body double, she plants a wet kiss on his sunburned scalp. "Monkey see, monkey do."

Albert seizes the moment, breaking away and performing his best chimp impression, hopping around and digging at his armpits while making grunting noises. He's relieved to see a smile break the harshness of his wife's face. "Ooh-ooh ah-ah," he says, milking the moment.

Even after all this time, he lives his life treading on eggshells, doing his best not to anger the woman he pledged his life to, but he guesses most marriages are like that, and it's just the way it is. At least it always was in his family: the woman in control, the man keeping his mouth shut and doing as he's told. A quiet life of servitude, rewarded with explosive moments of excitement. The marriages that last, endure the decades like he and Margaret have, are the ones that recognise and play by such rules. As he feels another tear escaping, he clutches at his wife again, watching gravity go to work. "They're my favourites, is all."

"Of course. We'll get some more, dear."

Albert's sometimes challenging; he knows that, but Margie mostly puts up with his funny little ways, or *monkey business* as she calls it. Without her, he would most likely be living in some crappy old people's home that smelt like piss, playing snap with folks wearing shit-stained underwear pulled up to their necks, hoping for the love of Christ that they're the next to go. "Promise."

"I promise, Alby."

And they have so much history. He contemplates all the wild things they've done, the games they've played that would make even the Devil blush. Knowing the best is yet to come, he licks his lips. "And some of those swirly things too," he says, "The red and white ones that that girl was eating earlier. I checked her pockets, but she didn't have anymore, and I felt sad."

"Okay, my dear. We'll get the swirly ones too, just for you, Alby."

"I love you, Margaret," he says, the ringing in his ears finally fading to a low hum.

"Love you, too, monkey."

"I like monkeys."

"I know you do, Alby; I know you do. You showed at that cottage last year that you can fling poop with the best of 'em."

Albert finds himself laughing. "I did do pretty good, 'specially when that turd hit the ceiling fan, gave everyone a shower it did." His smile fades. "Chimps are smart as people, though. And an orangutang can rip your arm off without even trying."

"I know, Alby; I know. You've told me all this a thousand times before."

"I'd like to rip someone's arm off before the curtain comes down."

"The night is young, dear."

Rain begins pelting the glass, and the wind ramps up its tempo. With his head still pressed against his wife's bosom, Albert watches the trees dancing and the ever-changing shadows of the canopy along the driveway. It's wild and temperamental out there, unpredictable, just like his Margie, and he feels a twinge of excitement that makes his penis jump in his pants. "Still don't think anyone will come tonight," he says, watching the torrent pelt the windows of Beatrice's Bed and Breakfast.

"Pip-pip, Alby. Make a wish."

Albert screws his eyes half-closed, willing for the sight of headlights. It's a big place for just the two of them, and besides, he'd like the opportunity to crack open the special brandy they picked up earlier.

"Did you make one, dear?"

"Uh-uh."

Perhaps a little conditioning, maybe the fact she keeps life a little interesting, but it's safe to say Albert loves his wife and would do anything to please her. The memories they share are nourishment, keeping his few remaining brain cells alive and kicking.

"Good boy."

Cancer is all over him, just like *Daddy* was when he first taught Alby what a beating was. Those were memories he was alright with losing. The way that old bastard took the razor to Mum and didn't even have the decency to kill her. He sat in the hospital for days while they tried to put her back together. Old drunk bastard didn't play by the rules in the end, and that's why they fell out and kept trying to kill each other. Albert kept that in mind when he met Margie and fell in love. Margie was strong like Mummy was, still is, and she has a heart full of gold.

Another blanket of wind wraps around the house as lightning flickers, basking the room in starkness. The branches of the trees beat against the house like the knocking hands of visitors.

"See, dear," Margaret whispers into his ear. "Someone's listening."

They stay like that for a while, eyes on the window, watching the rusty sign in the distance swing back and forth. They're too far away to actually hear it, especially over the howl of the wind, but Alby imagines the squeaking of the chains. It's a calm, peaceful sound that offers a not unpleasant feeling in his stomach. His mind provides a flashback of Mummy gritting her teeth as she pulled a bike chain tight around Daddy's throat from behind, the old man's eyes bulging like a puffer fish. It's a memory he hopes he holds onto until the end.

"I hope so, Marge. I really hope so."

Clock's ticking, though. And he doesn't want to be a burden.

The B&B was Margaret's idea, but Albert jumped at the opportunity, thinking it would be good to meet more people while he still could, creating more memories while the old ones faded from existence. Margie knew what he needed; this was all for him. She took good care of him, not just the kind of care she took her teeth out for but the kind that made your soul feel warm like a bug light after a fresh kill.

"Are you hungry, Albert?"

Thunder rattles the place with a boom, sending the trees into another interpretive dance. Albert imagines monkeys swinging branch to branch, chattering excitedly between themselves, also hyped-up on the possibility of guests. No longer in uniform, stark bollock naked, he's in the trees with them, cooing and screaming, his undercarriage dangling behind him like a stubby tail.

"Starving, dear. Maybe the storm will drop a cow off for us like in the movies."

Margaret laughed, a phlegmy choking sound. "Or something even better, my love."

—1—
Chris and Judy

"Smell that air, love," Chris says, tapping his wedding ring against the wheel in time to the music.

Judy lets out a relaxed yawn and slinks further back into the car seat. "Cow shit."

"I mean all the other stuff: the flowers, trees, mildew. I think I'm even getting a bit of honeysuckle." In his element, he begins singing along to Heartbreak Hotel, the music feeding through to his legs. "Well, since my baby—"

"You're such a loser, Chris." She squeezes his thigh to stop the annoying jiggle. "But I love you. How much further?"

"Not sure. Pass me that bottle of water, will you? And another one of those tasteless biscuits you made."

Giving him a sharp elbow on the way past, she stretches into the back for the square Tupperware box. "I don't remember it taking this long last time."

Chris takes a sip of tepid water and winds the window down, his gaze drawn to the seemingly endless tree line continuing into relative darkness ahead. There's a flashback to being a kid, imagining what wonders such wooded areas might conceal, what else might be living among them without their knowledge. A magical fawn, a terrible troll, or maybe both in warring factions to own the woodlands and support their princess. He once conjured a monster that still haunts him to this day, a half-human, half-tree hybrid that slowly crawled out of a breathing patch of earth in the ground, the top layer of dirt rising like a lid. It tried to speak but only released a series of sickening, coughing moans of choked-off syllables like someone whose mouth was filling with dirt as they tried to call for help. All he could make out was his name.

"Chris. Chris, are you listening to me? I said I don't remember it taking this long."

He still recalls the nightmares so vividly. That clearing—lit by a slither of moonlight, the warmth running down his legs as the rustle of its leaves got ever closer.

"And those clouds don't look friendly either. There's a storm coming; I know it."

Black eyes, so cold; the first of its shoots wrapping around his left leg, another snatching around his right as he screamed for his mummy and dug his fingers into the soft earth as he was dragged towards the blackness. And his cries, nothing more than garbled nonsense as he was yanked into the hole, the roots tightening further, snaking around his limbs and neck.

And then the lid started to close.

"Chris, watch out!" Judy screams, her grip clamping down on his leg.

Chris snaps his head back to the road, the car performing a quick shimmy as he tries to get his bearings again. "What the fuck, Judy?"

"A bird. I thought you were going to hit the little thing. You were going straight for it."

"Jesus and Mary, you sent my heart through the roof." A silly childhood nightmare that has stayed with him. Inexplicable, ludicrous, yet one he knows has made him claustrophobic ever since.

"Where were you anyway?"

"In a hole."

"Of course you were." She's used to his constant daydreams, the way he phases out mid-conversation, nodding like the Elvis bobblehead on the dash, but his mind entirely elsewhere. He's always been like it; she's often thought he should have been a writer, not an accountant. "I was saying it looks a bit mean over yonder, doesn't it?"

"It did say patchy rain on the forecast," Chris replies. Just the previous week, he was at the office, his last before early retirement. Bitter-sweet for sure, full of trepidation and melancholy. The first few days of so-called freedom didn't allay his fears, getting under Judy's feet every five minutes, until he put his foot down and insisted on this impromptu trip. Met with resistance at first, Chris tried to convince her it would be like old times when they would just get in the car and drive into the sunset, no destination in mind. She called him a silly old buffoon, but they eventually reached a compromise. They would drive to the coast and spend a few nights at the same hotel they stayed in for their tenth wedding anniversary. Same room, too. Judy had joked that his ticker might not cope with a repeat performance.

As the roads get windier and the sun slowly sinks behind them, they drive in comfortable silence, taking it all in, both capable of small talk but knowing they must pace themselves from hereon in and to their last breath. Rabbits tentatively emerge from long grasses, and crows feast on their dead relations. More tasteless biscuits are consumed, even a couple of pieces of celery, just for the sake of it, dipped in peanut butter to try and disguise the blandness. The saltiness leads to thirst and more bottled water left too long in the sun.

"How long now, Chris?"

"Not sure, love."

"What does the sat nav say?"

"I'm not using sat nav."

"What do you mean, you're not using sat nav?"

"I'm using this." He brings the ratty, tea-stained map from between his legs. "Old school, dear. If we're going to do this like the old days, we need to do it right."

"Jesus Christ, Chris, that's probably about twenty years old."

"We never had sat nav in those days, Jude. Just you, me, and the open road, adventurers without *roots,* taking the world by storm. I want to feel that again, to rekindle adventure."

"Sod that, I'm plugging it in."

Chris instinctively reaches across, ripping the phone from her hands. "No, don't, please. I want to do this the old way. It's on my bucket list."

Judy snaps her head towards him, opening her mouth to give him a tongue lashing, the cusses reaching her eyes before her lips.

"Sorry, love," Chris croaks. "Sorry." The look on her face tells him that his grovelling has only just begun. "It's just that every day for the last few decades, I've known where I've been heading, what I'm doing, who I'm seeing. For once, my day isn't a list of tasks. Let's live life, yeah? Old-school it! Come on. You know who I used to be. Let me be that again, even if it's only for a moment."

Judy fixes her gaze ahead, the ominous darkness and occasional flashing stealing some *thunder* and replacing it with trepidation. Still, she folds her arms and offers a sharp sigh to prolong his guilt. "Nothing wrong with routine; it makes you accountable for your time." Hoping it's just something to get out of his system, an adjustment to their new life, she decides to let this little jaunt slide. She closes her eyes, the hypnotic and gentle patter of the first drops of rain soon inducing her nose whistle.

Before long, the windscreen depicts a kaleidoscope of greys, greens, and browns. Only a smattering of farm animals breaks up the monotonous scenery and the occasional driveway marked by old tyres emerging from between a decrepit fence line. As Judy adjusts in her seat, letting out a squeaky little fart, something she's often prone to do while sleeping, Chris spies an old rusty sign to his left swinging wildly on the breeze. He's just able to catch the words 'Beatrice's Bed and Breakfast' before the wind flicks the sign up and out of his eye line. Ahead, something else catches his eye, but it turns out to be an old piece of tarp erratically making its way across the road. Hairs begin to prickle on his neck, their day no longer scripted, the approaching storm only adding to the mix.

Old school, baby!

Eyes getting heavy, Chris sticks his head out the window, letting the now much cooler air rush over him and the rain splash against his skin. The angle of it makes it feel like the tongue of a golden retriever happily lapping at his face, something he remembers fondly from childhood. His little ally— always there for him after one of his nightmares. He spies the water on the road ahead, and as if by the click of someone's fingers, the downpour escalates, the wipers struggling to keep up, even at maximum tempo. He quickly winds the window up, yanking his arm inside and stretching his eyes wide, but it doesn't help, the heaters blowing hot air directly into them no matter how he positions the small plastic lever. Visibility is bad enough with the rain, but if his contacts dry out, there's every chance they'll hit some poor *cow* safely going about their day.

Don't you dare touch that heater, his wife's voice sings in his head. *Right. Fuck.*

Concern builds as the rain intensifies, water spraying either side, at one point, creating a mini-fishtail that demands his complete focus, his fingers tightening knuckle-white around the wheel as he brings the car under control. Another flash basks the rain-drenched road, and for a moment, Chris thinks he sees the tree monster crawling out from the verge. The image blinks away, followed by crashing thunder that snaps Judy's eyes open.

"Chris?"

"It's okay, Judy." But the goosebumps lining his skin fail to back up his words. Still a couple of inches on the map between them and the hotel, the clouds showing no sign of breaking ahead, he knows what's coming.

"I don't like this, Chris." Judy clears her throat and adjusts in her chair, noting the stolen daylight and the lack of time between the rolling thunder and flashes of light.

"If it were just me, I'd keep going, but—"

"Yeah, and that's why married men live longer. Do you seriously think you would be alive now if I didn't get you to settle down? You'd be lying in a ditch or buried underneath a giant tree in an unmarked grave the way you were going."

"That's not even funny."

"No, it's not. That's why we need to find shelter somewhere."

"There was a B&B a few miles back," he says, slowing down further, his uneasiness growing at the sight of empty glistening tarmac ahead and behind. "We'll turn back, wait it out."

"What about the hotel?"

"I'll just tell them the truth. Hopefully, they'll just move the booking back. This is what I wanted anyway, right? Living life on the fly. What's more exciting than trying out a new place on a stormy night? It'll be fun."

Judy's never been the B&B type, all fuss and dust, but she supposes it's better than sitting on the car roof, waiting for emergency services. "I guess we've no choice."

"Excellent."

They make a turn using the next available driveway, Chris smiling at the thought of some Elmer Fudd type sprinting down the puddle-drenched path, carrying a shotgun and an empty bottle of moonshine, yelling at them to stay off his land. *Can I offer you a biscuit, Elmer? How about some flaccid celery sticks?* "Don't worry," he says, patting Judy on the leg, "You'll still get lucky."

"Chris!"

It's further back than he remembers, and just as Chris begins to think they might have missed it in the ever-worsening weather that they find themselves caught up in, the silhouette of the sign appears ahead. He watches it get caught in a gust of wind, sending it spinning end over end. Breathing an internal sigh of relief, he lets his head fall back against the rest. Only 4:15 pm, yet it feels like dusk as they pull into the driveway of Beatrice's Bed and Breakfast, gravel crunching under the tyres, wipers thrashing frantically.

About ready to feed Chris with more reminders of their lacklustre stays at such places, Judy's mood also picks up as she spies the top of the stone building between the overgrown hedgerow, wisps of black smoke emerging from the stately chimney and dissipating against the dull sky. Another flash of lightning draws her attention to magnificent red ivy weaving its way around golden brickwork and the warm yellow light leaking from windows onto a gravelled path that seamlessly turns to huge fields in all directions and a wooded area beyond.

"It looks quite nice," she says, deciding to let up a little, continuing to run her eyes over what could be a scene from the Catherine Cookson book she's reading. After all, it was Chris who arranged all this and whisked her away at a moment's notice. Very romantic, if truth be told. And she supposes she could do with letting loose a little. Their clashing dynamic but ability to meet somewhere near the middle made them work well. "Rather beautiful actually."

Chris brings the car to a halt, and they sit there for a while, soaking it all up as rain drums at the roof. Feeling victorious, he reaches over and pecks his wife on the cheek. "The fun doesn't have to stop just because we're getting on, Jude. I'll get the case."

It's getting chillier, but the glow from within, the smell of smoke in the air, and whatever's cooking provide warming nostalgia. With the suitcases buckling behind, Judy slides her hand into Chris' as they make their way to the door, heads turned left against the iciness. She pauses briefly under the porch, hairs bristling on her neck, mostly from the chill but also some anxiety at being out of her comfort zone. Not hearing a chime as she rings the bell, Judy follows up with a gentle tap, stepping further into the small circle of sheltered illusory warmth. She feels quite young again, the night ahead impromptu, unrehearsed. This is what Chris had been trying to tell her, and she can't help but look at him with a twinkle in her eye, biting her lip again as she does.

"Love you, Jude," Chris whispers. He knows he can be child-like at times, stubborn to the core. "No walk in the park," she once referred to him, but she plays tunes with her nose and ass when the moon comes out, so give and take, he figures. Besides, she looks good even standing outside in a downpour with windblown hair, half asleep. It's a reminder of just how lucky he got.

As hushed chatter emerges from behind the door, followed by footsteps, Chris clears his throat, unconsciously squeezing down on his wife's hand. She shoots him a half smile and squeezes back. With a heavy moan, the door opens, making Chris wonder if they are at a B&B or paying a visit to 1313 Mockingbird Lane. He doesn't voice the joke, knowing Judy to be uncomfortable enough already.

An elderly couple greets them, both hunched over, impossibly white teeth stretched into inane smiles. The woman is curvy, to say the least, skin stretched across rosy-red cheeks covered in too thick blush, arms like a shot putter, and a colossal behind that extends way back into the kitchen. She's wearing a pink frilly apron, *World's Greatest Grandma,* woven into the fabric. In contrast, the man's face resembles a walnut, his bony fingers wrapping around the door frame like twisted time-worn branches, sallow skin hanging from bones like washing on a clothes rack. His head is bald and spotted like a toad, and his eyebrows resemble obese caterpillars, the eyes underneath cloudy and pointing in different directions. Chris wonders which eye is good, deciding to focus on the left one, figuring he has a fifty-fifty chance.

It's an awkward stand-off, the old couple remaining silent, standing in the doorway and observing Judy and Chris as if they were two Royals dropping by for a surprise visit.

Unable to bear it any longer, Judy gives another sharp squeeze on Chris' hand and pulls it away, offering it to the odd couple stooped before them. "Hi, I'm Judy; this is Chris. The sign out front said you had a vacancy." She offers the warmest smile she can muster on this freezing night.

The woman nods, nostrils flaring, her breathing rapid and erratic. "Yes! Yes!" She wraps both her calloused hands around Judy's. "I'm Margaret. Call me Marge." Her eyes are cloudy and impossibly wide. "Albert, don't just stand there; get the case," she barks gruffly. "These poor folk are getting sodden."

The old man nods and shuffles past her ample behind to reach towards the handle, his back offering a series of crackles like burning kindle.

"It's okay; I've got it, Albert," Chris says, extending an arm between the old man and the case.

Margaret offers a sigh and rolls her eyes. "Don't pander to him, dear; he's quite capable. Unless that is, you're looking for a gigolo. Ain't much lead left in his pencil, if you know what I mean." Margaret sees the look on Judy's face and responds with hoarse laughter. "I'm only joking, dear. I'm sure you got no need for my Alby, what with the handsome young gun you have standing beside you."

Chris grabs the case, ignoring the awkward interaction. "The sign says Beatrice's B&B out front."

"Yes, Chris," the old woman replies.

"But you said your name was Margaret."

"That's right, Chris." The woman's smile widens, extending from one red cheek to the other.

"Okay then," Chris concedes. *Glad we cleared that up.*

Margaret nods. "Well, don't just stand there in the cold. Come on in. We want you to feel right at home. Mi casa es su casa." The old lady ushers them in, her big arms slapping against each other. "Learnt that in Spain, didn't we Alby?"

"Uh-uh," Alby replies, his face lighting up at the thought of all those lovely senoritas.

First across the threshold, an eyeful of strangeness as her reward, Judy takes in the house's interior. It's as if the walls are bleeding a watery discharge of blood, pink undertones everywhere, occasionally interrupted with drab art, colourful doilies, and an extraordinary collection of objets d'art. "It's—lovely," she says, turning to Chris.

Running his eyes over the décor, Chris feels like he's just walked into Elvis's parlour. He performs a little pelvic thrust, sweeps his thinning hair back, and curls his lip at Judy, who offers a smile. "Uh huh huh," he says in his best Elvis voice.

"Have you had a long journey?" Marge asks, eyes darting between them both, gesturing to the chairs by the fire. "You both look ever so tired."

"A few hours, yes," Judy replies, lowering onto the edge of the leather, the warmth from the fire already stinging the left side of her face. "We're supposed to be coast side by now, in a nice five-star hotel, but my husband took us the scenic route." She realises her insensitivity too late, noting the old woman's crumpled frown. "But it's brought us here, and that's just fine with us. This place has a cosiness that I'm sure no big hotel would be able to muster." She punctuates it with a smile, hoping it helps the elderly hostess to forget her previous remark.

"That's right, my girl. Put the kettle on, Albert," Marge commands without matching Judy's gesture.

"Pardon, dear?"

"Kettle, Albert!" She gives him a sharp frown, eyebrows like two pieces of iron wool almost meeting in the middle. They remind Judy of a car wash, an expectation that when they finally part, the skin beneath will offer a shine. She bites back a chuckle.

"Yes, dear." Albert begins to mosy along, his joints popping like microwave popcorn nearing its finish.

"Actually, Margaret, Marge, Margie dear," Chris jumps in. "Would you mind if we went to our room and freshened up first? Got that groggy car feeling going on, you know. We can get some dry clothes on too. I imagine it would be a nicer introduction."

"Of course. Oh, goodness, look at me, all over you like bloody monkeypox." She starts slapping herself on the wrist, lightly at first, but working into a bit of a frenzy, mumbling under her breath, spittle beginning to shower the air in front. "Silly old goose, Margaret. Silly old goose."

Albert begins spinning a finger around his right ear, prompting Chris to look at Judy and gesture towards the door. She shakes her head and purses her lips, a bolt of thunder crackling around them as if reinforcing her sternness.

"Silly old goose, Margaret. Silly old goose." An element of awareness returns that self-flagellation isn't part of social etiquette, nor likely in the guesthouse owner's handbook, but this only gets Marge more worked up and further ashamed. "Silly old goose. Silly old goose. Silly old mother-fucking goose. Fuck you, Margaret!"

"Cuckoo," Albert says, following with a cackle of laughter. "Cuckoo, cuckoo. I'm a monkey, and she's a cuckoo bird. Welcome to the animal farm."

Chris gestures towards the door again, this time with more venom in his eyes, but Judy's lips flatten further, suggesting no early escape from this *cuckoo's* nest. Besides, the only alternative is sleeping in the car; he can't imagine what that would do to their arthritis-ridden bodies. They're not quite up to Alby and Marge's state of decay, but they're far from being in their prime.

You wanted adventure, Judy silently mouths to him. "Honestly, Margaret, we're so happy to have found you," she says softly. Initially thinking Marge the saner of the pair, Judy figures the competition well and truly wide open again. "We really do appreciate your hospitality; it's just been a long day, and I think the chill of the rain might be going to our brains."

"Yes, I'm sorry," Margaret says, cheeks flushing to almost the same colour as her beaten wrist. "What must you think of me?" She puts a hand to her head, perching on the edges of one of the dining chairs. "Only we—" she takes a couple of deep breaths, "—don't get that many visitors, do we, Alby?"

"No, dear, but don't think that means the candy is old because it isn't."

Chris feels Judy's eyes on him, but he can't stop the words emerging. "You're a B&B, though."

"That's right, Chris, that's right." Marge grins, nodding profusely, eyes wide and watery.

"But you just said before that you don't get many visitors?"

"Well, we only get the odd passing guest, out in the sticks and all that." A series of crackles emerge from her throat as she straightens. "That makes sense, Chris, doesn't it? I think it does, but do you, Chris? Do you think it makes sense? You seem the analytical type. What's your logical brain telling you?" Her grin widens, gums glistening in the light of the fire, her dentures loosening in a spot, lending Chris thoughts of them spilling out onto the floor and continuing to chatter on their own. "Chris? Cat got your tongue, Chris? Chris? Ch—"

"Thanks, Marge," Judy intercepts. "Thanks so much for welcoming us into your beautiful home."

"Pleasure, darling. Now, let's see; the storm made it dark early. It's thirty-four past five now. How about we serve dinner up at seven dead."

"Oh, Marge, there's no need," Judy says. "We really didn't expect—"

"Nonsense, dear. I wouldn't be able to sleep at night if I let two weary travellers go without food for the night. I've got two big meat pies in the oven, and it ain't no beef doing some extra taters and veg. Alby will sort it." She clicks her fingers and pokes a fat finger in the side of his skinny frame. He jolts straight, producing some crackles of his own. "Yes, dear."

"Now, let's get you two lovelies to your room."

They make their way up a staircase that creaks even more than the hosts' bones, their feet sinking into the heavy-duty pink runner. Pink walls on either side leak onto the landing and into the narrow corridor unsurprisingly carpeted in thick pink shag. Sickliness also waits for them in the room, a long pink rug resembling a rolled-out tongue, ready to swallow them whole. Chris musters a smile, thinking back to his childhood retriever once again.

"If you need anything, just shout for Albert. Only shout loud as he's as deaf as a log." Margaret stands at the door, rubbing her hands. "Otherwise, We'll see you at dinner at seven."

"Dead," Albert adds.

Well, that gives me the warm fuzzies, Chris thinks.

"Thanks, Marge," Judy manages to say, just before Chris eagerly closes the door on the old couple's manic grins. He throws the case on one of the beds and slumps beside it, waiting for the footfalls to fade.

"I'm so sorry, Jude," Chris says, running his eyes around the room.

"It's fine," she says, plunging into the pinkness beside him. "It's—quaint."

"It's horrible. Where's the TV, for Christ's sake? And single beds, too?" He spies the Bible on the bedside table, and on either side of the bedposts, a small plastic Jesus on a cross. Centre stage on the far wall, a woven plaque carries the header, *The Lord's Prayer.*

"Poor fucking Albert," Chris utters as he walks towards the window.

Judy smiles, joining him, feeling the cold draft across her arm. "Nice view, though." Even through the dullness, it's magnificent, the window offering a well-needed escape from the pink—a thousand shades of green and brown as far as the eye can see. And aside from a decrepit and rather charred looking outhouse adjacent to a dam, no other building in sight. "It's perfect."

Chris moves his attention to the bed, sliding his hand between the mattress and the frame. "Here, give me a hand with this."

"What on earth are you doing?"

"I hate these bloody blankets," he says, groaning. "Squeeze the life out of you while you sleep. Can't stand them." The vein in his neck begins to pop as he wrestles with the heavy fabric, tearing it from each corner and fold, stomping across the room like a gladiator. "My Grandma used to have one just like—" Foot catching in its thickness, Chris goes down, tangling himself in a world of pink.

Surprising herself with a sharp guffaw, Judy doubles over. It sets Chris off, too, hysteria building until they're both red in the face, tears streaming from raw and tired eyes.

"It looks—" Judy inhales, trying to take back some self-control, but she's off again, more rasps following as she doubles over, unable to get the image out of her mind. "It looks like you're trapped in a giant vagina."

Chris reaches for her, carefully bringing her down into the soft fabric vulva. "The clitoris is over here," he says, grabbing a handful of the blanket. "That's why you married me, right? Because I'm a man who actually knows that?" They laugh again, like children, as they haven't for some time. A night full of surprises and a couple of crazies meant it was panning out to be just the adventure they needed.

"It's going to be a good trip," Judy says. "Thanks for organising it."

"Don't thank me yet."

They don't unpack; there seems little point for one night. They wash, change into dry, comfortable clothes, kick off their shoes and squeeze onto one of the single beds, letting their eyes close.

Chris smiles to himself. "Did you know that some people fart in their sleep?"

"What are you talking about? Is that your attempt at romance?"

"Forget it," Chris says, a mischievous grin spread across his face

"You've gotten weird since you retired."

"I don't want to be one of those couples, Judy, walking the dog wearing matching anoraks," he utters.

"We don't have a dog."

"I know, and I don't want one. Especially not one of those little rat dogs like Clive and Fiona have."

"Aw, Barney's cute," Judy defends. "Look, I can't promise I'll jump out of planes with you or swim with sharks, but We'll compromise wherever possible, okay?"

"That's fair. I did enough of that for both of us already. Besides, we already have our list."

Judy smiles, resting a hand on his ample chest. "This is fun, though. I'm having fun."

"Me, too," he says, snuggling closer. "I'm going to lose this weight, too; I promise." He rubs his stomach, and they giggle as it jiggles like jello.

"Dog-walking's good for that."

They lay there for some time, holding hands, not asleep but in a state of calm, wondering what the years ahead may bring. There's renewed optimism that this could be a new beginning, not the ending they were both dreading.

"Fifty-two past six," Chris finally says.

Judy offers another snicker, instinctively gazing over her shoulder towards the digital clock radio on the randomly white doily, numbers a pinkish hue. "I think my eyes are bleeding."

"Shall we go? Engage in some witty repartee with Tweedledum and Tweedledumber?"

"They're kind of sweet," Judy replies. "Just their way, I guess. Old-school is the quote of the day, I believe."

"There's old school, and there's the walking dead. How on earth is that man still alive? Every time he moves, his body plays a tune."

"You'll be that age one day, love."

"I bloody hope not." Chris pushes himself from the bed, giving the discarded blanket a swift kick and feeling the sometimes-forgotten twinge in his leg. Whether he likes it or not, age is catching up with him. "Hey, do you remember that Irish guy that played the bones? It was our third anniversary, I think, in Dublin."

"Your brain connects dots I never would, but I remember. The wind caught his kilt, and for a moment, I questioned whether or not you were straight the way your eyes popped."

"It was bloody massive."

"Your jaw hit the floor."

"So did his dick."

Judy laughs. "Come on. We don't want to be late."

Chris is overcome with the temptation to flop into the bed again but knows Judy wouldn't let him get away with it. "Alright. As soon as we've had dinner, though, we make our excuses, okay?"

"I'm not going to be rude. You know me better than that." Judy ushers him to get the door. "Besides, this storm doesn't look like it plans on letting up. We're here until morning whether we like it or not."

Chris turns, fingers wrapped around the door handle. "The code word is pink," he whispers. "We bail out after that."

"You're such an idiot. I should have run away with the Irishman."

Chris shows her a mock offended gaze and then leads the way down the hallway, feet sinking into the thick shag as though it's nothing but marshmallow. Stopping dead at the top of the stairs, he almost pokes Judy in the eye as he swings an arm back.

"Chris, what—"

"Shh. Look."

Peering over his shoulder into the living room below, Judy squints as if what she's seeing must be a trick of the eyes. In front of a colossal rear-projection television that broadcasts only fuzz, Marge is embedded in a pink chair, her chunky spider vein legs extending onto a pink frilly footstool, pink cup and saucer gently rising and falling on her bosom. Albert stands directly behind, slightly to the right of the large grandfather clock, hypnotised by the same static screen, his fingers raking through his wife's hair. Every so often, he brings them out, pinched together as if carrying something.

"Pink," Chris utters, watching Albert tilt his head back and release the catch of the day into his open mouth. He urgently tries to usher them both back, but Judy isn't ready for his about-turn, and they end up tangled in a knot, momentum taking them into the pink wall. A framed picture of a young girl and a rabbit having tea rocks above them, falling crooked.

"There you are," Marge cries, wide eyes and glistening gums pointed towards them. "Perfect timing." She groans as she pushes herself from her entrapment. "Albert, serve up, dear."

"Yes, love." He hobbles towards the kitchen, Marge following close behind, rubbing her hands as if trying to set them alight.

"You knocked my elbow, clumsy fool," Judy mutters on the way downstairs.

"Sorry, love, but didn't you see the show?"

"They're just old. Funny little ways."

"Funny little ways? If I scratch my back with a fork, you go ape shit, pardon the pun."

"Idiot."

"Maybe I should set up a tyre for them in their yard."

"You'll never be funny."

"So it's romantic? It's settled then. I'll groom you like a chimp when we return to the room."

Judy ignores him.

"And beat my chest and throw poo at you."

"Aw, can't we do something different?" she says, surprised how much she's enjoying the childish banter.

The table waiting for them in the kitchen holds no surprises: pink tablecloth, pink mats, two large pink candles sporting a pinkish-looking flame, and even pink knitted covers for the salt and pepper shakers.

"What's your favourite colour, Marge?" Chris asks, prompting Judy to stick another elbow into his side.

"Her favourite colour is red," Albert chimes in, following with a cough. "It was Beatrice who loved pink so much."

Marge shoots the old man a scowl, thrusting the pointy end of a rolling pin into his rib cage. The old man doubles over, but Marge grabs the collar of his shirt and drags him back up.

"Old-school romance," Chris whispers to his wife.

—2—

Richie and Melody
(Earlier in the day)

"Tell me why we're doing this again?" Melody asks. Her crossed-over bare feet hang out the passenger side window of the van, toes decorated with glittering blood-red polish, a silver anklet with an ankh dangling from her right ankle. She's eyeing the black clouds that appear to be on a collision course with them. "Why can't we just stay in a hotel like everybody else?"

Richie smirks from behind the wheel, head shaved on the side facing her, the other side draped into a long purple mane stretching to his shoulder. "This is how I see it, babe. Hear me out, right. We only live once, so with that in mind, you should spend your whole life checking things off your bucket list, making sure you do everything there is to do. Really living, you know?"

Melody licks her cherry-red lips. "I don't think staying at a shitty B&B in the middle of bumfuck nowhere is on anyone's bucket list, Richie."

"It's on mine," he says, leaning forward to turn on the wipers now that the black clouds have finally decided to unleash. "I've been meaning to see more of the country for a while. Sick of the sight of concrete, and besides, I need some new song material. Might go for a bit more of a chilled-out vibe for the next one."

"Sure you will!"

"Hey, I've got a sensitive side."

"Sensitive like Gacy at a children's party. But seriously," Melody says, pulling her feet through the window and scowling at the water that comes inside with them. "Why?" As she hits the button, the window offers a gentle scream of protest, beginning its slow journey upwards.

Richie laughs, leaning in towards the wheel and taking a drag of the cigarette that juts from his fingers. "Because I've never done it."

Shaking her head, Melody reaches over and snatches the cigarette from him. She sucks from it, returning it to his fingers with a cloud of smoke. "It's a B&B, Richie, not heroin."

"I've already done heroin." He takes the last drag and flicks the butt out the passenger window a split-second before it seals. "Yeah! Indiana Jones'd it, baby!" He holds his hand out for a high-five, but Melody knocks it away.

"What was it like?" she says.

"I didn't care for it, to be honest, but I wrote a kickass song while I was on the shit, just to see if I could. Crossed that motherfucker off my mother-fucking bucket list."

"Lovely," Melody says with a yawn. "Richie, you're twenty-nine; you shouldn't even have a bucket list."

Richie chuckles and shakes his head. "Babe, you never know what's going to happen. We can die tomorrow for all we know. Look at goddamned Tommy. He was younger than me."

"Tommy was an idiot and drove over a hundred in the rain."

Richie gets a devilish look in his eye, and Melody knows what it means. She hates it. They're due to get married in a month. "Riche, no." The man sitting next to her is about to become her forever, but she can't help but think every time she catches that look in his eye, forever isn't going to be very long. It doesn't sit well. Cold feet, perhaps. Fucking freezing actually. But she's a sucker for his charm and knows resistance is futile.

"Richie, please. Not in the rain."

"I've never done it."

"For once, can we keep it that way? Don't you want to make it to your Bed and Bucket List?"

"Just for a second," he says. "To say we've done it."

Before Melody can voice her protest, his foot pushes down on the accelerator. The van takes off, flying faster than she ever thought it capable. She screams, punching him on the shoulder, while Richie laughs hysterically, the rain beating on the windshield, matching her blows in a rhythm of synchronised violence.

Heart still racing, Richie finally eases off the accelerator and lets out his breath. *This is what life is all about.* He slaps his hands repeatedly on the steering wheel and offers a "Whoop!" He's just done what killed his best friend but came out the other side, blood pulsating in his ears and the lyrics of his next song already forming in his head.

"That was for you, Tommy. Fuckin A!"

He can feel Melody's eyes burning into him. She gets fed up with him sometimes; he knows that. But one thing's for sure; he wouldn't want to experience such a rush without her at his side. He can still recall that moment when he caught her backstage trying to steal his gear. Immediately, he knew that she was the one, that she would be with him for the rest of his life, however long that turned out to be.

"You're a fucking asshole," Melody finally barks, her face as white as a sheet.

"Yeah, but I'm your asshole."

She snorts, turns away, and sits on her knees, grabbing her pleated skirt by the waistband. Squinting into the pelting rain, she presses the button, patiently waiting for the window to come down. "Nope," she says, sticking her buttocks through the gap and her tongue out at Richie. "*This* is my asshole."

"What the fuck, Melody? It's fucking freezing!"

"You're right." She turns in her seat and shakes her rain-soaked ass in his face. Richie moves his head away, sending the car into another swerve on the rain-slicked road. "What the hell?"

"I've never done it," she says with a sly smile, tugging her skirt back up and righting herself in her seat. Feeling smug, she sets the window on a course upwards and shakes off some of the rain.

Richie returns the smile and slaps the steering wheel again. "That's why I know you're the one, babe! A match made in Hell. Yeehah!"

They spend the next few minutes riding in silence, Melody smoking and still gloating, Richie focusing on the road as the weather continues to worsen, visibility reduced to a few yards as relentless rain bombards from all directions. The wind begins pushing and pulling at the car, screaming like the ghosts of the damned, impossibly loud through the closed windows.

"Getting pretty bad out there," Richie finally says.

"Pretty bad? That's like saying Hitler was a slight inconvenience." Melody studies her future husband, thinking it's as though Evil Knievel has just been possessed by a little old lady, the way he's now holding his hands in a perfect ten and two, leaning over and squinting through the rain-flecked windscreen. *Maybe he really does want a future,* she thinks. *Maybe he really does care for me. Is this the soft side he was talking about? Why do I never see it?*

"What made you like that anyway, Richie? A sensation seeker." She's asked the question in other ways before, but the barriers have always stayed down. The last time she tried, she came close, but on the verge, he closed up again, locking himself in the back room pretending to work on another song. But this could be the moment, she figures. This could be the moment to bond them stronger than ever. "If we're going to get married, I want to understand you, really understand you."

Colour draining from his face, Richie offers her a glance before gluing his eyes back to the road. He sighs, shifting uncomfortably in his seat. "Don't like to talk about that to tell you the truth, Melody. But seeing as though you is you." He lights up another cigarette and takes a drag. "When I was a kid, Mom left me on her friend's porch, said she forgot something and would be back in five. Needless to say, I never saw her again."

Melody notices the cigarette shaking between his fingers as he brings it to his lips and takes a long drag.

"Cried until it hurt, but real life ain't like the movies," he continues. "People don't just take babies they find and love them, turn them into heroes. I was turned over to the authorities and put in the system—went through foster home after foster home 'til I ended up with a psycho named Rita who liked using me as her ashtray. A punchbag, too, if she was having a bad day. But that was just the tip of the fucking iceberg."

"Jesus, Richie."

He remembers being dragged into the crawl space, left in the cramped darkness as the door slammed shut behind. Seconds turned to minutes and then hours. "Nightmares last a couple of days at most, but that stuff stays with you, Melody. It's in your skin, bones, hair, and heart. Fucking bitch." He recalls pounding the door until his fists hurt and his voice went hoarse, the taste of blood at the back of his throat. But the woman who was supposed to mother him stayed away, leaving him there until the dark became solid and choked him, shadows becoming shapes and every noise a monster. Crying in the darkness, nothing but ghosts for company, he used to wish himself dead. He can still taste the earthiness and feel the cobwebs on the side of his face. Finally, his eyelids would win, and he would wake up back in his bed with a more sober Rita serving him fresh, cold, homemade lemonade.

"You start life going through things like that, and it's enough to break you," Richie continues, "Never to let you be happy." As nerve endings in his fingertips scream, he frantically presses at the window switch, letting out a small yelp as he tosses the butt. "But if you think of it all as a set of experiences, sensations, it somehow makes it okay. You start seeing everything that way."

Melody exhales quietly, reaching over and putting a hand on his thigh. "I get that," she says solemnly. "I was never in the system, but my real momma wasn't much better than your Miss Rita. My grandparents cared for me most, but I never got much love from them, just the chills." She thinks back to that one incident with Grandpa. "Your grandpa just had a funny turn, is all," Grandma had said.

"Fuck 'em," Richie says. Immediately craving a distraction, he reaches for the pack of cigarettes again. "Pass me the lighter, will you?"

She retrieves it from the centre console and hands it across. "Smoking'll kill you."

"Funny girl." He blindly reaches out, grabs it, and sparks a flame on the first go, bringing it to the cigarette dangling from his lips. "Just call me The Fonz, yeah?" But just as leaves begin burning, the cigarette slips from the corner of his mouth, landing dead centre of his crotch. He lets out an un-Fonzie-like high-pitched scream and reaches down, sending the front left tyre into the grass verge and the van shuddering.

"Richie!"

Cussing loudly, he wrestles with the wheel while brushing at the thin material of his pants. "Fuuuuuuuuck!"

Melody reaches over to help him, but the van jostles roughly as the verge swallows them further, slamming her head into the driver's side door. "Mel!" Richie cries out, looking down on his future wife as she moans in pain. The tyres buckle further still, prompting him to look up, his eyes growing wide, a garbled moan leaving his lips as he sees the enormous rock ahead. In desperation, he swings the wheel to the left, but the van is on autopilot now, taking them side-on towards the boulder. "Fuuuuuuuuuuuck!" Richie screams, bracing for impact.

An explosion of twisted metal and shattering glass jolts them violently in their seats and sends their ears momentarily ringing. But it's over impossibly quickly, relative silence falling, aside from the sound of steam pouring from the hood.

Melody sits up, holding a hand to her bleeding forehead. "Was that on your fucking bucket list, Richie?"

"I'm sorry," Richie says, lines across his forehead making him look older than his years. "I'm so sorry. You okay?"

"I'll live, but you might not."

"Fuck!" He pops the door open, thinking how the rest of his band will kill him. Too small for a tour bus, the van was the best transport they've had in years. "Fuck. Fuck. Fuck." He hops out into the rain just as lightning basks the puddle-drenched road. Rain pouring by the fistful, he lowers his head and offers the driver-side door a gentle thump.

Melody arrives beside him, her sandals offering little protection and her hair dishevelled and plastered across her forehead. With a hand still pressed against her temple, she reaches the other towards Richie's arm.

"Sorry, Mel." Feeling a level of love that he never thought himself capable of, Richie leans into her, thinking even after all the shit he puts her through, she's always there, to reassure, to comfort, to—

"I can see your dick," she says.

"What?" Shivering, Richie looks down to see the hole burned into the crotch of his pants. And there, unmistakably, is the tip of his manhood, poking out like a turtle's head, checking to see if it's safe. "Ah fuck! That's what you get for buying charity shop pants."

Cold to her bones, Melody's still unable to stifle a snigger. "Did you not check to see if the crotch was fireproof?"

"Funny enough, no," Richie replies, unable to stem his smile. "Besides, it's always an inferno down there."

"I don't know; it looks pretty cold to me."

"Oy!" Richie adjusts, tugging his briefs to the side to conceal the hole. "At least it was you and not Beatrice."

"Now what?"

Richie sighs as the icy wind finds its way to third base. "I don't think we're far now. We could probably just walk there, get the van looked at in the morning."

"The thing's a fucking piece of shit anyway."

"Might be the case, Mel, but we've got a show in a few days, and the guys depend on it."

Melody yanks the side door open, thinking the day can't get any worse. "Come on then, Magic Mike." With a two-handed grip, she begins pulling at the enormous suitcase.

"How's your head?" Richie asks, reaching for his own much smaller case. "It's bleeding some."

"I've had worse just being in the pit at one of your shows. Can we just get going?"

Richie nods and starts towards the road, his black suitcase decorated in tour stickers and band emblems bouncing behind him. Melody keeps pace, cursing herself for packing too much and not bringing sneakers. She'd ask to swap, but nobody—nobody—is allowed to touch Riche's band stuff.

As thunder booms in the distance, they both look up, catching a lightning strike not too far ahead. "This place better be cool," she says.

"It will be. The whole place is pink; you saw the pictures on the internet."

She did. Even the background was pink. "Shitty website, though, not even being able to book online. I mean, come on!"

"We're dealing with the nearly dead, Melody. The lady, Beatrice, is a total Bible freak. Even asked if we believed in God."

"And let me guess. You—"

"A-fucking-men, baby. I read a review on Yelp that her son is like the real-life Norman Bates, albeit an even skinnier bald version. All weirdly obsessed with her. There's a picture of him, too; the guy looks like a riot. It will be a hoot, Mel, I promise. I was all polite and shit on the phone, though, of course."

"Such a charmer."

"Exactly, but one look at us, and Beatrice is going to think we're bringing the devil into her house. It's going to be wild. The son's name is Ezekiel." He laughs, offering Melody a nudge. "Imagine what Zeke will think when our headboard starts banging against those pink walls."

Melody offers a sigh, her arms already beginning to sing.

As they arrive at the road, soaked to the bone and freezing, wet clothes feeling like armour dragging them down, they turn their attention to the rusty B&B sign spinning around a wood post in the wind. Richie performs a little hip wiggle to keep the rain from tickling his pecker. "God, I'm looking forward to a hot shower and a change of clothes."

Cases buckling as they catch the potholes, they start towards the guest house, flicking the bird at the disappearing tail lights of a trailer that sends a tidal wave of brown water across them.

"Fuck this," Richie says as they finally leave the blacktop, venturing down a dirt road into a maze of endless trees. Beautiful any other time, the scenery is now just another part of this terrible experience. Finally, they arrive at the front door, gathering in the orange glow like moths to a flame, shivering as their clothes cling to their skin. Lips chattering, Melody brings an almost translucent hand against the wood, wincing at the feedback.

The door creaks open almost instantly, revealing a hunchbacked and shrivelled old man with awe-stricken watery eyes, one pointing east and one west.

"Tell me this isn't the son," Melody says.

Richie shrugs his shoulders. "Hi. I'm Richie Omega. We have a reservation?"

"Oh my," the old man says. "The chocolates were supposed to be for you, but I ate them." He fixes his stare on Melody's sandals, eyes almost bulging from his head. "I can't remember if I put more out, silly old monkey. I can give you those swirly ones that are minty too, but they're not chocolate. Is that okay?"

"We just want to get out of this rain," Melody responds. "Not really in the mood for candy."

"Jesus, Paul, and Ringo, Albert. Let the poor folks in. What's wrong with you? Can't you see they're freezing?" Richie and Melody hear the voice before they catch full sight of who it belongs to, unable to see anything but the woman's rear end jutting out like an extendable table. She wraps a big hand around the old man's arm and yanks him aside, revealing her grey curls and intense eyes embedded deep in a cherubic face. Most of her top and bottom half is covered in a large apron advocating her as 'The World's Greatest Grandma'. Richie finds himself contemplating what that even means—imagining a hypothetical world championship for such a thing. A bake-off, perhaps? Cleanest dentures? Biggest knickers? Most cans of flat soda in the cupboard? A smile beams between two large circles of bright blush, making her look like an old porcelain doll aside from the contrasting blemished skin. "Welcome," she says jovially. "How can I help you?"

"They have a reservation," Albert chimes in.

The old woman's eyes light up as though checking off the winning lottery numbers. "Oh, of course. How could I forget!? I tell you, my old noggin isn't what it used to be." She moves forward with remarkable efficiency, Chris likening it to the shuffle-version of speed-walking. "Richie, yes, and you must be—" she eyes the young girl up and down— "must be—"

"Melody."

"That's it. Melody. Richie and Melody sitting in a tree, F-U-C-K-I-N-G."

The young pair exchange looks, Richie biting his lip, thinking Church folk as nutty as a fruitcake mostly made from nuts. He watches Albert take his suitcase and move to get Melody's. "You must be Beatrice," he says to the old woman who wobbles in behind them, closing and bolting the door, blocking out the furious storm.

"If you say so," she says with a smile. "I can see your pecker."

"Shit," he says, moving his hands to cover the hole that had worked its way back over.

"Don't worry, petal; I've seen it all before," Margaret says, ushering Melody into the warmth and bringing her lips towards the young woman's ear. "Not bad for a starter, but what do you do for the main?"

Melody shrugs, snapping her head towards Richie.

"So... are you?" Richie persists.

"Who?"

"Beatrice."

"You can call me Beatrice if that's what you like. Alby calls me all sorts when the sun goes down."

Jesus wept. "Okay, Ma'am," Richie croaks.

Melody's unable to hold onto her snigger this time, but as she catches the old guy staring at her feet again, licking thin lips all cracked and pale like the moulted skin of a snake, her amusement fades.

"Just fooling with you, son. I'm Margaret or Marge. Albert calls me Margie sometimes, but you ain't him, so don't." She offers a burst of laughter, cutting off abruptly and leaving the foyer in awkward silence. "There's another couple in the upstairs room, so We'll put you two downstairs. Albert will show you where it is so you can get dried off and changed. I'll put in some extra stuff for dinner."

"Honestly, that sounds amazing," Melody says. "I could eat a whole cow right now."

"Oh, petal, did it not say on the website?" Margaret says. "This is a vegan B&B. They're jack fruit pies in the oven."

Drenched through and nothing but paper-fucking-mache for dinner to look forward to, Melody flicks a scowl at Richie. He returns the glare with 'I'm so sorry' puppy dog eyes, but they provide little consolation.

Another bolt of explosive laughter perfectly synchronised with rumbling thunder catches Melody off guard. She snaps her attention back to the old woman who's now doubled over, shoulders heaving, hands on her swollen kneecaps. Between stands of frizzy grey hair, she can see some nobbled skin, reminding her of those knotted loaves of bread she sometimes passes in the local bakery. Caught up in the excitement, Albert offers another one of his chimp performances, beating softly at his chest and sticking his tongue out.

"I'm just kidding, petal." Marge finally straightens, her blusher smeared across her face, her eyes like runny eggs. "You should have seen your faces!"

"Very good, Bea—I mean Marge," Richie says, wanting to get as far away from the maniac as possible.

"And should I set another place for your little friend?" Margaret says, drawing her stare back to the torn fabric between Richie's legs. "Or has he already eaten?"

"Yep, another good one, Marge," Richie says. He continues his retreat, following Albert, who hunches over even further as he drags their suitcases down the hall. This is definitely something most people won't experience in their lifetimes, Richie thinks. *Checking boxes for sure.*

Melody offers the old lady a glance, considering asking her where Beatrice is but decides she'll ask at dinner. The last thing she wants right now is to start what could be a long conversation, listening to more of the old lady's riddles as she stands there sopping wet and shivering. Hugging themselves against the chills, the young couple study their pink surroundings, a stale smell of wood and old things filling their nostrils, reminding Richie of the crawlspace, and sending a shudder down his spine.

"Dinner is at seven dead!" Margaret shouts from behind.

"Dead," Albert says, turning to look at them both, an eye on each. He stands the suitcases up on either side of a doorway. "Here we are."

Richie and Melody watch him hobble away like a beaten tortoise before finally offering each other a look, a smile at the corners of their mouths.

"Shall we?" Richie says, holding onto his laugh until he figures it's safe to release. He opens the door and steps into the room, finally letting the cackle go. Mouth hanging open, eyes darting around the room, Melody follows.

"Holy shit."

"What did I tell you? Pink. Every fucking where!" Richie laughs again. "This place is gonna be wild."

"It's hideous," Melody tells him as she strips her wet clothes off on her way to the bathroom. "As if a pre-school girl designed the fucking place."

"I'm gonna write a song about this. I'll call it 'Not So Pretty in Fucking Pink.'"

"I'm taking a shower before it's seven dead. Care to join me?"

Richie's smile widens. Something about fucking in strange places really turns him on. The tour of the old jail back home when they snuck off into one of the cells, the graveyard last month under a full moon, and now this phallic place of worship under the guard of 'The World's Greatest Grandma' and her pet chimp. Without bringing the cases in from the hall, he slams the door shut and starts ripping at his wet clothes. "Hell yeah!" His eyes move over the only non-pink things in the room—the brass crosses on every wall, each one with Jesus nailed securely, head hanging over his chest. Richie chuckles to himself. "Let the sinning begin," he yells, bounding naked into the bathroom.

Offering Richie a naughty grin, Melody opens the door to the shower stall. He follows closely behind, the warmth and wicked thoughts causing his wrinkly little pup to stretch out from between its fleshy pillows and restore to former glory. As he embraces her, steam rising around their nakedness, he momentarily thinks he sees the water turn pink but figures it's just his eyes playing tricks. "We're sorry, Beatrice. Or Marge or whatever the fuck your name is," Melody says as she shuts the door behind them. For just a split second, she thinks she hears a soft creak and the faintest of whispers. *You will be?* But as the pipes offer a rattle and a hiss, she puts it down to her being tired and the place old. "Worth the walk," Richie says, his manhood already standing firm as he presses his lips against her neck.

Refreshed and spent the best way, they finally step out of the shower. Melody grabs a fuzzy pink towel from the nearby rack and wraps herself in it, intending to drag the cases from the hall. Behind, Richie sings one of his songs and pulls the towel harshly back and forth across his back and shoulders.

"Richie."

"What? What is it?"

She nods towards the suitcases leaning against the bed.

"I left those in the hall," Richie says, stepping up beside her, his pink towel dropping to the pink floor. Not a fan of *anyone* touching his band stuff, he decides the old couple weren't to know and gives them a free pass this time. "I guess they brought them in for us."

But Melody's only half listening, her mind once again conjuring the throaty voice of the old woman in her head. *You will be. You will be. You will—*

"Shit, it's almost seven," Richie says, drawing Melody's attention back. Just pipes, she thinks. *The hiss made to sound like a whisper. It's just old people creeping you out, Mel.*

"You okay, Mel?"

"Yeah." She glances over at the bright pink wall clock, pink hands ticking by a picture of a smiling pig. 6:57. *You will be. You will be. You will be.*

Richie can already hear the muffled conversation. "Well, come on then."

"I'm ready," she mutters, finally putting it down to her imagination and her traumatic childhood. She keeps her distance from *oldies* wherever possible, not enjoying the thought of being so close to death. And their hosts have hardly helped, their gummy smiles, wild eyes, and—*you will be*—bizarre personalities. And didn't Richie mention something about a son? Her mind boggles trying to comprehend what sort of freak would emerge from such courtship.

—3—

Dinner

Chris and Judy are already at the table by the time Richie and Melody make it. The guests exchange glances, a knowing resignation to whatever the night has in store.

"Sit down, my lovelies," Margaret hollers from next to the stove. "Albert, get a move on, for goodness sake. The guests are hungry. Can't you see they're hungry?"

He grimaces as he bends over, reaching for the oven handle with a rattling groan. "Yes, dear."

"Did you remember to put a cross in the pies as I asked you to?"

"Yes, dear."

"And in the sprouts, too?"

"Yes, dear."

"Oh, Albert," Margaret says, poking at the contents of a large pan with a wooden spoon. "This broccoli's ruined; the colour's all washed out, and it's as flaccid as your—"

"I'm Chris, and this is Judy," Chris says, thrusting his chair back urgently and offering a hand. "Hell of a storm, eh?"

"No need to stand, dude," Richie says, wrapping his tattooed-covered fingers around Chris' small, soft hand. "We're not the fucking Beckhams."

"Richie," Melody scolds, digging him in the side. "Nice to meet you," she says, offering her hand to Judy. This is Richie, and I'm Melody." She knows she'd never be top of the class at charm school, but she does know manners and that people don't expect to be fleeced by well-spoken folk. "And yes, it's horrid out there."

"Yes, it most certainly is quite awful," Richie mocks. "Chills one to the bone." He wishes he had a drink in his hand so he could thrust his pinky out.

Judy offers him a smirk, thinking she likes the kid already. Like a younger, slightly more feral version of Chris before she got her mitts on him. "I like your tattoos," she says, feeling her skin prickle even as the word tattoo leaves her lips.

"Thanks. You should see the one on my—"

"So," Melody interrupts, releasing Judy's hand and offering Chris' hand a shake. "What brings you to this world of pinkness this evening?"

As small talk resumes and the couples exchange accounts of their journey, Albert wipes the sweat from his brow and begins dishing out. Every part of him lights up with pain, but there's an even greater ache deep within, not in his bones or his weary muscles, but in the dark part of his mind reserved for special moments.

"Nice big helpings for our guests, Albert," Marge instructs. "Oh, it's so nice to have people for dinner. Get the good wine, too, Albert!"

"And the brandy?"

"And the brandy, dear."

"Yes!" Albert yells, almost dropping a pie in excitement. He groans and reaches into the cabinet above, bringing out a bottle with a posh-looking sticker.

"I don't suppose you have any Scotch around the place, do you?" Chris asks. "I think it's a night for it."

Judy offers him a kick under the table. "We want an early start in the morning, though, Chris, don't we?"

"Just a little one, for warmth."

"Scotch is a dessert drink," Richie chimes in. "We need clear liquor with dinner."

"I'm afraid no Scotch, dear," Marge remarks. "Wine, brandy, or tap water are your choices. The last folks used up all the clear liquor, didn't they, dear?"

Albert whispers something under his breath, but none of them catch it.

"It's a beautiful spot," Judy offers. "Chris often says he'd quite like to move into the country. Never could with work, but now he's retired, too, I'm not averse to it."

"What do you do all day, though?" Melody says, directing her attention to the old lady. "Nothing around for miles."

"Oh, we find ways of keeping ourselves entertained, don't we, Alby?"

The old man nods and offers a gummy smile. "Games, all the best games."

"Well, don't just stand there, Albert. Let's go! Let's go!"

"Yes, dear."

He begins slicing up the pie and delivering a portion to each plate, spatula shaking frantically. Each time the pie makes it to its destination, Judy breathes a sigh of relief.

"Smells so good," Richie says. "I could eat the scabs off a tramp's head."

"Richie!" Melody scolds.

Chris shoots Judy a look, recalling the incident from the tops of the stairs where Albert appeared to be grooming his beloved. He tries not to imagine what goes on behind their closed bedroom door. After thinking nothing could be scarier than the patch of breathing ground that has stayed with him since childhood, he considers he may have found a fitting replacement. He lets out a little shudder, praying sleep takes him quickly tonight and has the mercy to be dreamless.

"Oh, did you ring the hotel, love?" Judy asks.

"I did," Chris replies. "While you were getting a shower. We're not the first to ring."

"Was that the Vue Grande?" Melody asks, putting on her posh accent again.

"That's right," Judy replies. "Lovely place. Just on the side of an artificial lake, surrounded by a field of lavender." She catches Marge giving her a stern look, immediately making her cheeks tingle.

"I wanted to stay there, but Richie said he wanted to do rural properly."

"Yeah, like what's the going rate for a kidney these days?" Richie says. "Besides, this place is perfect: remote, log fire, a home-cooked meal, even a free light show."

"I agree," Judy says, in full-rescue mode. "Quaint." There's that bloody word again. If quaint translated to looking like the inside of a coffin and smelling like shit on fire, she thinks.

"They're a bit weird, though, aren't they?" Melody whispers.

"I like 'em," Richie says. "A couple of sandwiches short of a picnic, I'll give you that, but I bet they've stories to tell, some real rock n' roll shit."

Chris leans forward, enjoying the interaction with new friends. "They look like they've been around the block more times than a kid with a new bike." It was a phrase his dad used to say, one of many that never fails to induce a sigh and a roll of the eyes from Judy, today no different.

"Yeah, but I think they're on their final lap now," Richie says, fumbling with the pepper shaker. "Fella looks like a gust of wind will blow him over."

"Fucking hurricane wouldn't take her down, though," Chris adds, feeling rather pleased as he observes the smile breaking across Richie and Melody's faces. "And I'm sure that fucking mole on her chin winked at me before."

"Chris!" Judy snaps, despairing at her husband's attempts to impress the young kid.

He even surprised himself with the cuss, but it felt good to Chris, freeing him somewhat from the shackles of expectations. He decides he might even throw another *fuck* in before the night's out. Perhaps two, three, maybe six, he figures. This isn't the time for bed socks, hot cocoa, and Sudoku; this is a night of strangeness—new surroundings, new people, the storm of the century outside. *Fuck it all!* But as he catches his wife's stare, his balls contract, and he's the reserved retired accountant once more. "Sorry, dear." Momentarily, he tries to imagine what Judy would say if she found out he'd been taking antidepressants for most of their married life. "Sorry. Sorry."

"At least they made it that far. We almost bloody died on the way here," Melody says.

"But we didn't." Richie gives the metal horns with both hands, his face quickly souring as he contemplates the repercussions again. "Fucking van did, though."

"That sounds terrible," Judy says, eyes wide. "What happened?"

Melody tells a short version of the story, Chris and Judy *oohing* and *aahing* in the right places, Richie feeling at once embarrassed but fearless. He senses a little bit of envy from Chris and guesses the man's tidy haircut and the starchy shirt are just part of the act, a way to blend in with all the rest of the cast of this fucked up world.

As Albert serves up the veg, relative silence falls, apart from a huff, puff, and a loud crackle from Marge as she lowers herself into her seat. Chris studies her, trying to get a read, flickering lightning only reaching half her face. He's usually quite good at analysing people—*You seem the analytical type*—but he gets nothing from the old woman sitting across from him, redundantly wearing an apron sporting the bold claim.

One by one, plates are planted in front of them, the smell stirring stomachs and diminishing the storm that still rampantly performs around them. Richie picks up his fork, but Melody offers him a sharp kick and a cough.

"Hurry with the drinks, Albert," Margaret yells.

"Yes, dear."

"You had an accident?" Judy resumes.

Richie grins. "A rain-soaked road, a lit cigarette, and leather pants."

"Fake leather," Melody adds.

"Christ," says Chris, immediately cringing as he receives another scowl from Judy. "I mean fuck. I mean—"

"Brandy, please," Richie says to the old man, never having tried the stuff. As soon as Albert finishes pouring, he picks up the glass and knocks the drink back, offering a grimace and a shudder as it slides down his gullet like warming cough medicine. "I guess it's an acquired taste."

"Only one way to find out," Albert says, offering that impossibly wide smile again and refilling the glass. He doesn't mind sharing the special brandy on important occasions, and what occasion is more important than this? This is one for the ages, one for his bucket list.

"I'll take a wine, please, Alby—I mean Albert, sorry." Melody watches the old man tilt the bottle, his hands shaking, the wine miraculously finding its way into her glass. She guesses he's used to working under pressure, though, being married to the battle axe two seats down.

"Guests first, Albert," Marge says, brushing him away and sending him towards Chris and Judy. "The teeth stay in for the selfish."

"Of course. Sorry, dear."

Richie can't contain himself, a muffled snigger emerging. Melody wants to play Judy's game and scold him, but she's too busy bottling her own laughter.

"Thanks, Albert," Chris says, bringing the glass of red to his mouth almost instantly. The deep red liquid is half gone as he sits it back on the pink coaster, sending some splashing over the side. Ignoring yet another scowl from Judy, he figures He'll make the best of things. "Fill her up, Albert!" *Fuck you, Judy. Tonight, we're gonna rock n roll.*

"With pleasure."

"Back to what you were saying before, though; it is a very quiet life," Margaret says, leaning forward. "We don't even have a phone, so intrusive I find them."

Judy watches the bottle trembling in Albert's hand. She prefers white but hasn't the heart to tell the poor old fool. "Thanks, Albert."

"Takes a bit of getting used to," Margaret continues softly. "We were ready, though. It might not look like it now, but we knew how to have a good time." She leans back in the chair. "The stories we could tell, eh, Alby?"

Albert finally takes his place at the table. "Yes, dear. Would make their toes curl." He smiles like a gleeful child, reliving more fond memories.

"Salt and pepper, Albert!" Margaret commands, forcing a groan from the old man as he wearily gets to his feet again. He almost immediately goes down, grabbing the back of a chair to steady himself.

"Wait," Richie says, his mind playing catch up. "You said you don't have a phone."

"That's right," Margaret replies.

"But I spoke to you last week—to make the reservation."

"That's right, dear."

"On—the—phone."

"Yes, dear. We had one then."

"Riiiiiiight."

"Well, eat up then," Margaret says, clapping her hands together, prompting a mild ringing in Melody's ear.

Richie picks up his fork again, but the thought won't leave him be. "But won't it be tough running a B&B without a phone? I mean, how do you get any bookings? You can't book on the website; I tried."

Melody finds herself wondering where the son is. *Perhaps he was the one who put the cases in our room?* A shiver runs down her spine at the thought.

"Oh, you're an inquisitive one, aren't you, little Richie. What with you and Chris over here, it's like Friday night down at the bingo hall with the blue rinses." She offers another manic laugh, slapping a hand on the table, jolting Chris and Melody in their seats. "A couple of old ladies, chattering about nonsense over the fence. Hark at her, hark at him. She did what? She never did. Well, stone the fucking crows."

Albert breaks into hysterical laughter, banging his palms on the table hard enough to rattle the plates and send wine sloshing from Judy's glass.

"Baby Ruth!" Richie yells, following with a snigger. Melody covers her mouth, unable to stifle the giggle and the words, "Goonies never say die."

Chris and Judy laugh along but haven't a clue at what.

"It's Richie's favourite film," Melody says, sensing the confusion. "He's nothing but a big kid."

"Baby Ruth! Baby Ruth! Baby Ruth!" Albert yells, prompting another round of giggles from Richie and Melody.

"Fuckin' perfect," Richie says.

As things settle, Richie wants to return to his line of questioning but lets it go. And after Marge's little outburst, Melody has also decided it's likely best to keep a lid on their curiosity. They continue exchanging a series of bemused glances, Chris unable to help thinking Alby's reference to an animal farm didn't do the place justice. With a nervous cough, Judy reaches for the wine bottle while thinking of a way to break the awkwardness. She opens her mouth to speak, but Chris beats her to the punch. "Did you want to say grace first?" he says, aiming his attention at Margaret.

Richie sighs and puts his fork down again while Margaret offers Chris a blank expression, her mouth opening and closing almost mechanically, like a child's chomping robot.

"I saw the Bibles upstairs and thought it polite to ask."

"Well, that's very considerate, Chris, but Alby and I think one's faith is very personal. Feel free to lead if you like, but we prefer to keep that sort of thing separate."

Richie opens his mouth, ready to ask the relevance of their earlier question to him on the phone but decides better of it, thinking nothing about these bloody country folk makes any fucking sense. He's never set foot in a church or uttered the word 'Amen,' and neither is on his bucket list. Not to mention that he's fucking starving, his groaning stomach relentlessly reminding him of the fact.

"So go ahead, eat," Margaret starts up again. "Anyhow, the country is great for those who have almost finished with their living. Like one big and beautiful waiting room, isn't it, Alby?"

"Yes, dear. Just a few presents left to unwrap before the curtain comes down."

Judy waits for the old man to sit down again before cracking open the generous chunk of pie, noticing the young kid's cheeks already as full as a squirrel's. "This looks amazing."

"It is. It really is," Chris sputters, a globule of chewed pastry finding its way onto the table. "So good."

"Jesus Christ, that ain't bad," Richie says, forking another mouthful in. "Tender, juicy, just like Mother never used to make. The bitch."

"I love it," Melody says, loading her fork.

"All local produce," Margaret says. "Fresh is best we find, don't we, dear?"

"Fresh is best," Albert concurs. He picks up his fork, but it slides from his knobbly fingers, hits his calf, and lands with a clatter under the table.

"Clumsy old fucker," Marge says, eyeing her husband with disgust. "Like living with a bloody toddler. Only the other day he fell off the toilet, arms and legs in the air like a bug and shit everywhere."

Richie momentarily pauses chewing, his mind filling with nastiness. The lyrics to *Geriatric Shit Parade* begin to form in his mind.

"Albert, let me get it for you," Judy says, pushing her chair out.

"Ah, ah, ah," Margaret says, wagging her swollen finger. "Albert's more than capable, Judy. We mustn't pander."

The old man groans as he gets to his hands and knees. With a little squeal, he disappears beneath the frilly pink tablecloth.

"More drinks, anyone?" Margaret says, more than pleased with the way things are going. "That big old storm can kiss my ass."

"It kissed Melody's before," Richie comments. "Right on the—"

"Sprouts," Melody says, offering her fiancé a look of daggers and lifting the tray towards the centre of the table.

Family is the natural progression after small talk, and Chris and Judy gush about their kids and how their eldest, Catherine, expects in September. Margaret talks about her four sons, all married with their own kids and all with nearby farmland. It's all very pleasant.

"Are you alright under there, Albert?" Chris says. "Do we need a search party?"

"Got it," the croaky voice comes from under the table. "Just takes me a while to get up."

"You can say that again," Margaret says, slapping her hand on the table again and offering her cacophonous guffaw. "Needs a run-up sometimes, don't you, love?"

Chris squirms in his seat, trying to conjure the tree monster as the lesser of two evils.

"I think I'd like to have a child," Melody says, surprising herself with the revelation and looking across at Richie to gauge his reaction.

Richie almost chokes on a lump of potato. He can feel his eyes watering as he swallows hard, trying his best not to be a dick about it. It's something they've never really discussed, perhaps both not wanting to tarnish what they have by exploring too far into the future. There was an assumption, though, that after all the trauma they both endured as kids, neither would want to be responsible for another human being. He also assumed that was why she chose him, the opposite of a father figure: a train wreck, a ticking time bomb, a wannabe rock star, the anti-fucking-Christ. He swallows a generous mouthful of brandy, trying to imagine how a child would fit into his live-fast-die-young lifestyle.

The more Melody thinks about it, the more she convinces herself she wants to be a mother. Perhaps it's the wine, perhaps the projected wholesomeness of the crazy old grandma wearing the apron, but she feels funny inside, even more so as she catches Richie's watery eyes. "Not now, Richie, but at some—" she recoils, feeling something wet brush across her toes. There it is again.

"Melody?" Richie says, still with a proverbial lump in his throat.

Albert springs up on the other side, wearing a smile and holding his fork in the air like a trophy. "See."

"Good boy, Alby," Marge says.

"Thought I—" Melody watches the old man begin to dribble a potato around his plate. "Must have been a draft." She's sure she can still feel wetness on her toes, though, her appetite suddenly dwindling. *Your grandpa just had a funny turn, is all.*

"Seriously good pie, Marge," Chris says, washing another mouthful down with a swig of wine. "Any chance of getting hold of the recipe?"

"I could tell you, but I'd have to kill you," she replies in a deadpan tone.

"Worth it," Richie says, already halfway through and working more onto his fork. "Hey, where's Zeke, by the way? You kill him and bury him in the yard with Beatrice?"

"Who?" Margaret asks, screwing her face up.

"Ezekiel, the weird-looking fella on the website. He's supposed to live here with Beatrice. And where the fuck is Beatrice anyway?"

"Oh," Margaret says, offering a toothy smile. "Don't worry, dear. They're around. You'll meet them soon enough."

"Wait," Chris says, mid-chew. "Just before, Alby said pink was Beatrice's favourite colour."

"That's right, Chris," Marge says.

"Was being the operative word. So that made me believe she was dead, and you two have taken over the place."

Marge's gums widen. "Did it, Chris?"

"It did."

"Chris reads a lot of spy books," Judy interjects, sensing the tone. "Retains information well. Used to think of himself as James Bond back in the day."

"Well, James," Marge replies. "It could also mean Beatrice has simply found a new favourite colour. Or that Beatrice has moved onto a new business, leaving her old legacy with us."

"Which is it then?" Chris asks, swallowing hard.

"Why don't you tell us, Mister Bond?"

"So you play music?" Judy asks Richie, tearing through the atmosphere.

"He's actually amazing," Melody says, the music in her voice displaying her love for him.

Judy's eyes widen as she slakes her elbows across the table. "Anything we'd know?"

Richie laughs. "Yeah, I'm sure you probably keep the track 'Unholy O Face' on repeat as you drive to le super Marché."

"Well, it's cool that you make music," Judy tells him. "Anything creative is good for the soul, I'm sure. Even your unholy orifice, Richie."

Chris sprays the tablecloth with wine, his eyes streaming as he plays his wife's words back in his head. So prim and proper, butter wouldn't melt; this is a scene he will take to the grave.

"Unholy O Face," Melody corrects through her laughter. "It's actually really good. It's about—"

"I like music," Albert says.

"Alby plays the kazoo like nothing you've heard before," Margaret says, clapping her hands. "He'll have to play for you later."

"Oh, I can't wait to watch Albert playing his kazoo," Chris says, his laughter dampening as he catches his wife's stern eyes. She shakes her head and looks away.

As the conversation turns to nature, cars, food, and today's youth, Albert nods and grins in the right places, but Judy can't help feeling sorry for the old man. It's as if his mind is on other things, things that might soften or perhaps offer a coping mechanism for his apparent life of servitude and the automatic declarations of obedience that frequently emerge from his thin lips. She takes another sip of her wine, thinking once again she should stop giving Chris such a hard time. But she does not approve of his liberal use of the f-word tonight, thinking there must be some modicum of control. She gets that he wants to be free, but it doesn't mean he has to behave like a hedonistic teenager. *For God's sake, we're practically senior citizens.*

"Fucking amazing pie," Richie says, screwing up a pink napkin and running it across his face. "Might even have to write a song about it."

"Richie the musician," Marge says. "I always liked that one group. What was it? Jerry Lee Lewis and the News? What kind of stuff do you play, Richie boy? Rock, pop, country? It's not jazz, is it? I can make nicer music rifling through the cupboards—all over the damned place. Fucking stupid jazz. I like order, myself."

"More like giving orders," Chris mumbles. Frustrated, Judy throws down her crumpled napkin and gives him another, 'you're taking it too far' stare.

Melody sniggers. "It's death metal, Margaret."

"Deaf what?"

"Death metal," she says. "It's—well, it's—"

"Loud," Richie finishes. "Think of it as music to vent to." He turns his attention to Chris. "Looks like you could do to vent some," he says, flicking his eyes towards Judy.

Judy shoots him a glare. "Hey! I listened to Morbid Angel and Deicide in college; I just grew up."

Melody laughs and reaches across the table to give the other woman a fist bump.

"I have no idea what you're all talking about," says Marge. "Alby?"

"There's a band called the Monkees. I like monkeys."

It's the perfect end to a long day's driving, Chris thinks. He's enjoying himself much more than he thought he might, the food partly to thank for that, the company not as bad as first appeared, and the wine is going down nicely. Nice drop, a bit of an aftertaste, he thinks, but it's certainly helping him relax. Be nice if Judy did the same, he contemplates, wishing she would revert to how she started the evening. Anyhow, he figures they'll get an early night, and tomorrow, they can make their way to the coast. Not much traffic; that's one good thing about no schedule, not having to chase your tail.

"So, retirement, Chris. How are you coping with it?"

He finds himself wondering why they never have pie. Criminal, really. Something else for the list, he thinks, as he swigs back more wine.

"Chris!" Judy spits, self-restraint already caving to exasperation.

"Yeah?"

"Marge just asked how you are finding retirement. You know, the conversation we're all supposed to be having?"

"Oh, right." He swallows, feeling somewhat upset as he looks down at his almost empty plate. "Well, early days, I guess. We have lots of ideas, and now it's finally here, we certainly intend to start living it up."

"Why did you wait?" Margaret comments, chasing her peas around. "Until retirement, I mean. Alby and I have been living it up ever since we met."

"That's what I'm talking about," Richie says with a smile as he reaches over to take Melody's hand.

"Oh, I was a bit like our young friend, Richie, back in the day, wasn't I, love?" Chris says.

Judy nods. "Apart from the tattoos and the nose ring, yes."

"Offence not taken," Richie says. "Any more pie?"

"Albert, more pie for Richie," Margaret unnecessarily bellows.

"Yes, dear."

Judy feels herself blushing. "Oh, I didn't mean it like—"

"Just playing, Judy." Richie offers her a wink, thinking her quite tasty for an old bird. Would he? Really? She said she was around sixty. But a nice little black negligee and a bit of lippy. Yeah, he would. He watches more pie arrive on his plate, an urge to kiss the little old man on his bald scalp.

"Believe it or not, I was an Elvis impersonator back in the day," Chris continues, trying to take back centre stage. He curls his lip, flicks up his collar, and makes the sound. "Played a lot of gigs, even bought an old Cadillac and restored it. But kids, the job—ah, you know, life."

Richie makes eye contact with Melody, relaying his fears of ending up like the old grey-faced accountant, reminiscing about the good days, the middle part of his life eliminated, taken up with a memory dump of changing nappies and trying to get kids out of the door. The fear is real, emphasised by Melody's returning stare and pursed lips that indicate this is one thing she isn't prepared to compromise on. "Well, you're just an old hound dog," he says to Chris.

"You bet," Chris says, licking his lips as he receives more pie. "Going to make up for it now, though, aren't we, Jude?" he says, drumming his fingers on the table. "We have a list."

"We have a list, too," Albert says. He sits back down, back in the dark world, loudly drumming his knife and fork on the table.

"Albert!" Margaret scolds.

"Sorry, dear."

"Looks like we've all got a list," Melody says, feeling the effects of the wine. She reaches for the bottle on the table and drains it. "Doesn't mean to say we can't add as we go, though."

Richie ignores her, recounting the fingers on his right hand, as sure as shit that he sees six.

"Albert, more drinks!"

"Yes, dear."

The poor old bastard gets up again, nursing his back but knowing it will all be worth it.

"There are some lovely antiques in the house, Marge," Judy says, once again feeling for the old man.

"Nonsense, dear," Margaret says, dismissing her by wafting a hand in the air. "All the stuff you see here is worthless bric-a-brac. We keep the special mementos from our travels in a special place, don't we, Alby?"

"Special," he echoes.

"So you've—" Judy places a hand down on the table as it slowly begins to spin. "So you've—" Now, there's suddenly two of everyone, five more at the table than she could see before, and she's not sure which are impostors. "Travelled a lot," she finally manages to get out.

"All corners of the world, and some, dear."

"What's your favourite place?" Richie says, using his extra new fingers to aim the fork at the remains of his dinner but only striking the plate. The metal prongs scrape the ceramic with a high-pitched squeal, making everyone cringe. "I wanna go Texas."

Marge digs Albert with her elbow. "Fill their glasses, Albert."

"Yes, dear."

"The Amazon," Margaret finally answers. "We went in fifty-eight. Just bairns we were, really, only a couple of years over twenty. I was a nurse, and Albert was a journalist, see. Got us places other folks wouldn't even think of."

"Coooool," Judy slurs, unable to feel the right side of her mouth. "That place looks so—so—" She trails off, her words beginning to sound funny, as though she's speaking in an alien tongue. "Tree-y." Her subsequent giggle is interrupted by a random hiccup.

"I feel weird," Melody says. "Like I'm—floooooooating."

"Just need a red balloon, and we're laughing," Richie says, following with a burst of childish laughter.

"Anyhow," Marge says, rubbing her hands together as she does. "Tell me your greatest fears. I always think you can tell a lot about a person from what they're afraid of."

As the stunted, drunken conversation continues, Richie bursts into laughter, trying to stab a pea with his fork. "Yes," he jubilantly cries as he makes his catch, confusion returning as he continues to miss his mouth, finally lodging the pea in his right nostril. He lifts his head back, presses the other nostril, and fires the pea out, seeing perhaps a dozen of the little green projectiles leaving his nose towards the other side of the table. *Awesome.* He turns his attention to the others, feeling his lips moving but unable to understand the words coming out as though they're all running into each other.

"Juuuuude. You—alright, Jude?" Chris says, nursing a sudden sting on the side of his face. "Jude, wos matter?" He giggles, thinking his voice sounds like a chipmunk going through puberty. Letting out a snort, he raises a hand in front of his face, watching the lines begin to snake across his palm. "Woah, would you look at that?"

Albert is beside himself now, giddy. His legs tap frantically under the table, his pain secondary to the excitement. Warmth leaks across his right thigh, but it's not an unpleasant feeling. "I'll get more wine! I'll get more wine! Sleepy time's coming! Sleepy time's coming, Margie. Soon it will be time for the good games."

"The Am—zon." Judy says, trying to spring back to life. "Must—must been—have been—really—intesting." She finishes with a sharp guffaw that scares her, not helped by the sight of Margaret's gums that suddenly look bigger than ever as if consuming the rest of the face around them.

"Oh, it was such a fantastic adventure, wasn't it, Alby? The best of times. So many places, so many tales to tell. And so many wonderful people. We always brought things home with us, didn't we, Alby? Little keepsakes to remind us of the people we met."

"Like a whirlpoooooooool," Melody says, staring at the textured swirls in the ceiling as they begin to merge, the old woman's voice fading to nothing. "You see it, Richieeeee?"

But Richie is preoccupied, loading his nostril with more peas, firing them at the photograph on the mantel: an elderly lady wearing pink and a gentleman wearing a proud smile and one hell of a mother-fucking moustache. A younger man stands in front of them, who he assumes to be a young Zeke, wearing a bow tie and holding a Bible. The church in the background he recalls passing on the journey here, how its starkness was further emphasised by the flash of white, giving him prickles across the skin. Hardly any surprise based on the last song he wrote, 'Ass-fucked by the Devil.'

His first few attempts are a lacklustre effort, resulting in most projectiles finding the inferno's open flames that dance across the impossible number of logs. "It's a hell of a thing, killing a man." As Spaghetti Western music plays in his head, he decides it's time to get serious. He loads, inhales through his mouth, takes aim, and—*fire!* "Fuck, yeah!" Direct hit on the young fella just above the bow tie. He loads up again, aiming at the woman standing behind the young man's left shoulder. And—*fire!* Disappointingly, the pea lands a fraction to the left of her pink bonnet. "Your lucky day, Ma'am."

In the background, he hears someone shouting for help, but his eyes are on the man to the right of the woman in pink. In awe of the curly moustache, he loads the last pea from his plate and lines up the shot, gripping the table in an attempt to stop the spinning. "It's just you and me, son." He aims, he inhales, and—sends a stream of snot running down his chin and the glistening pea three feet short of the fire.

"Help, Richie!"

He quickly wipes the dampness away with the back of his wrist, snapping his head towards Melody to see the tablecloth dancing above her legs and her arms doing breaststroke.

"I'm drowning, Richie." She claws the air above her. "It's sucking me in." She slips off the chair onto the floor, letting out a series of garbled moans.

"I'll save you, my love," Richie shouts, ripping off his shirt and working at his faux-leather pants.

"—and the people were really welcoming, too," Margaret says, persevering through the tomfoolery, a million memories flashing through her mind. "Not like what we'd heard or thought." She rests her knife and fork on the side of the plate. "Really surprised us, didn't they, Alby?"

"Uh-huh. They had nice feet. Margie let me keep one." Albert returns to the table with another bottle, sliding another generous piece of pie onto Chris' plate and sloshing more wine into his glass. The old man opens his mouth to speak again, but Margaret steals his thunder. "We were young but old enough to be fairly cautious. Stunning place, full of amazing colours and wildlife, but we knew it could be dangerous."

"We like the monkeys," Albert offers, grinning and drumming his cutlery on the table once more as he takes his seat, prompting more sniggers from Judy. The old man stops as soon as Margaret turns her gaze towards him, but Judy is already past the point of no return, tears streaming down both cheeks, not helped by Melody and Richie's Baywatch reprisal.

"Not just the monkeys, Albert. Oh, it's such a shame we haven't more time, so many tales to tell. And we even have some photographs in our special place. There was this one time where—"

As the old woman's voice grows distant, Chris watches his wife push the plate away. She wavers left to right, comes full circle, and finally begins slowly falling headfirst towards the table.

"Timber!" Albert shouts, raising his spindly arms in the air.

Chris reaches his hand out, just managing to catch her head before it connects with the table. Inspecting his balloon-like fingers, he begins to giggle, which soon transitions to a full-on guffaw. And just as he manages to regain some composure, he sees Hasselhoff on the floor wearing nothing but a Tarzan G-string and bright pink socks, giving his fiancé mouth to mouth. *What a night!* He figures they'll laugh about it for years to come, perhaps not tomorrow or the next day as there will be a mourning process as they put their embarrassment to rest, some things needing to sit out the heat for a while to cool down. But what a story to tell the kids at the next family get-together, he thinks.

"—never forget our time there, will we, Alby?" Marge says, finally cutting off to take a breath.

One glass of wine. That's all that Chris recalls Judy having; even the way he was knocking it back wouldn't account for the spinning faces. Christ, he's gone through nearly half a bottle of Scotch before and still been right for work the next day. In his younger years, yes, but still—

"I said, we won't forget our time there, will we Alby?"

The old man's cough surprises Chris and prompts Judy's eyes to open again. Bony fingers wrapped around his kneecaps, Albert turns away from the table and retches towards the ground. "No, dear," he gasps, taking a handkerchief from his back pocket and bringing it to his lips. The speckle of purple tarnishing the stark white fabric doesn't escape Judy's attention. She thinks about saying something but is suddenly too exhausted to form words.

"Are you nuh eehing, Marge?" Chris says, noticing the untarnished pie and the old lady's untouched glass of wine.

Marge rests back in her chair, folding her arms and offering her gummy smile. "Looks like you're eating enough for both of us, Chris."

Chris turns his attention to Albert, noting his glass full and the pie intact. "Alber—nuh hungwy?"

"Oh, yes; starving," he replies, tapping the silverware on the table's edge again.

Judy's nose begins to whistle, and she lets out a squeaky little fart that has Richie in stitches. "Rock n roll," he says before his head crashes onto the floor next to Melody's.

"Anyhow," Marge sets off again. "It doesn't matter what you see or hear; you never really truly know who you're dealing with until you're up close and personal. Take Alby and me, for example. We might look as old and fragile—"

Chris watches her thin lips moving, the words drifting in and out, sometimes merging into nothing but a drone. He studies the other guests, eyes closed and mouths wide open, suddenly feeling quite proud he lasted the younger ones out. But he knows his time is coming, his limbs and eyelids inexplicably heavy, and the pink walls closing in around him.

"—can still show you young'uns a thing or two."

Unable to feel his fingers, he looks up at Albert and across to Marge, both staring at him, eyes wide, gums out. Their heads begin drifting towards the ceiling like released helium balloons, stopping halfway and spinning around each other, reminding Chris of a cheap seventies pop video.

"Sleepy time," Albert says.

Chris feels himself falling but has no response, hardly feeling a thing as his head makes a soft thud against the table.

"Let's get them tucked in," he hears Marge say before the tidal wave of pink finally takes him. "Make sure to get all their phones and wallets, my love."

Albert claps and gets to his feet. "Time to play."

—4—

The Game Rooms
Richie

Things remain dark as Richie opens his eyes. Pitch black. He feels a sudden surge of panic, a hand gripping his chest. He tries to move and hits a wall. Something to his right is blocking his way, too, and something behind presses into his spine. He reaches out blindly, tracing his way around his confines.

No. No fucking way!

"What the fuck? Hello?"

It's the crawlspace all over again. He tries to straighten, but the ceiling blocks any chance of relief from his aching spine. He tugs at his collar as though it's constricting around his neck. *What the fuck? What the fuck?* Struggling for breath, he imagines the shadows hiding within the blackness, the ghosts of the past returning to keep him company.

As the blood in his ears pulsates like the bass to one of his tracks, *Murder Monday,* he tries to stay calm, telling himself there has to be a door somewhere, a way out. If they got him in here, there must be a way to get himself out.

"Is there anyone there?"

Margaret and Alby's manic faces flash in front of him as he replays the parts of the night he can recall. He can still taste the brandy, but the fogginess in his head suggests something more than a hangover. Richie's had the best of them, some lasting more than two days, but this feels different.

They fucking drugged us. The old fuckers gave us something! I got roofied by the World's Greatest Grandma.

Disoriented and anxious, he feels like the child crouching in the darkness again.

Who the fuck are these people?

He can still see that wicked gleam in the old woman's eyes, the smile that was a little off and not just because her teeth weren't fixed in properly. He knows she must have been the mastermind, the ringleader to whatever this circus is. And the old man with the fondness for monkeys and playing the kazoo, dutifully doing as he's told, perhaps the promise of Marge taking her teeth out, the reward for such servitude.

But where did they put him? A crawl space with nowhere to crawl. He's crammed in and can't even stand up straight. "Fuck!" Panicking, he feels up the walls with trembling fingers, looking for crevices, hinges, cracks, anything that offers hope. Trying to control his breathing, he tries again, patting his hands more slowly against smoothness. *Come on. Come—*

He feels something.

Richie follows it around, his heart thundering against his chest. *A door?* Yes, he can trace the hinges with his fingers. He looks for a knob but can't find one. He pushes against it, but there's no give at all. And why is there no light getting through?

Because the fuckers have either sealed it somehow or put something behind it, you fucking genius.

"Help!" Richie screams, beating his fists against the wall. "Help!"

No way. There's no fucking way. Just a B&B, nothing more, nothing less. So why is he trapped in a room the size of a child's wardrobe?

Soon it will be time for the good games.

"Melody!" he cries, throwing himself at the wall.

Did they know somehow? What he'd been through, what he was afraid of? Maybe he'd talked when he was all messed up. We were all messed up. Who knows what he said, what any of them said?

He breathes quickly, trying to rationalise chaos. A million thoughts rush through his head, but he knows where this all leads, unsure if the old couple will show mercy and finally drag him out. What he wouldn't give for a glass of Rita's lemonade.

As panic takes hold, it feels like the walls are moving in, the house itself joining in the *games*, revelling in the absurdity. He imagines the huge front door they first entered as the gummy mouth, the large windows like big droopy eyes, lighting up on their approach, watching them, judging them. "Fuck you," he says out loud to the imaginary shadows. "And fuck you, too, you ugly old bastards! You fucking loons. You fucking coffin dodging, crinkly, watery-eyed shit-stains on human existence! Fuck you!"

He tries to control his breathing, knowing panic will get him nowhere and that Melody will be waiting for him. Even the thought of her being holed-up somewhere is too much. He lets out a garbled cry and punches the wall, a memory flashing in his head of driving a hole in the plasterboard of his friend's house a few years ago, a drunken disagreement about the best rock band of all time.

"I won't let you down, Melody."

Loading up, he takes his chances, grimacing in preparation before finally throwing himself at the wall. Pain reverberates across his shoulder and up his arm, prompting a high-pitched yelp and a feeling of absolute hopelessness. He tries in a different spot, punching, barging. He can feel his knuckles bleeding, the skin splitting between them.

"I'm coming for you, Melody," he cries optimistically. "Then We'll fuck up those two croutons good and proper." Another shoulder barge, and another, all with seemingly no effect at all, only to send more ripples across his right side. "You can't kill death metal. You can't kill death metal," he chants, trying to protect his dwindling spirits from the hungry darkness filled with the shadowy eyes of unerasable childhood trauma.

In desperation and in what little space he has, Richie begins kicking, grimacing as roaring fires of pain run up and down his legs and spine. As he tries to ignore the stinging pain, a comment he made last night flashes in his head. *You kill him and bury him in the yard with Beatrice?* Not so fucking funny anymore. "I'll kill you both, you crinkly fuckers," he cries, throwing relentless kicks and punches at the wall until his limbs are raw. "You're fucking dead. You've kept the worms waiting long enough!"

Rage taking over, he turns his attention to whatever other objects constrict his movement, punching and flailing at all in his path. "Let me the fuck out!" At one point, as things clatter to the ground, his right hand brushes across something smooth and round. Claustrophobia pinching at his airwaves, he inspects further, this time running his hands across fabric-covered hardness.

"I fucking hate mannequins," he screams, beginning to thrash at the wall once more. "Let me the fuck out!"

And from somewhere close, he hears something screeching across the floor, giving way to the muffled sound of laughter. The door opens slightly ajar, allowing a morsel of light, most of it still blocked by the burly woman standing on the other side, her snorting finally winding up.

"The fuck is this?" he cries.

"What's the matter, little Richie? Don't you like it in there, all snug as a bug in a rug?" Margaret shouts through. "I thought for sure you would like it. Snug as a bug in a rug. Snug as a bug in a rug. Snug as a—

"Let me the fuck out," he cries, reaching for her, just managing to get his arm through the gap. "Let me out, you moley fucking bitch!"

Before he can react, she clamps her big hand around his and brings his tobacco-stained fingers towards her mouth. "Think I can still smell her on you, Richie."

All he can do is watch as the World's Greatest Grandma, strong as an ox and twice as ugly, bites down hard on his index and middle fingers. He lets out a high-pitched scream, snapping his arm back into darkness. "Not my fucking fingers, you sack of fucking shit!"

"Oh, calm down. By the looks of the shit heap that you abandoned up the road, you're hardly going to be the next Jerry Lee Lewis."

"Let me out. Please just let me out."

"Maybe I will, eventually," her voice sings through the dwindling light. "Most of this is for my sweet Alby's benefit, but I had to cross at least one thing from my own list, you know? Saw this in a movie once, and it hit my good spot, if you know what I mean. Did one alive in the dirt before, but never in the wall, never like this."

"You're fucking mad," Richie states, darkness on him again.

"Oh, don't be like that. This is new and exciting, just the way you like it. Don't you like it, little Richie? Oh, say you like it, just for Grandma. Say it's rock 'n roll enough for you."

"You need help." He forces his fingers between his collar and throat again. "I'm a rockstar, man. People know where I am. I made a reservation. You're going to go to goddamn prison for this."

Hoarse and throaty laughter pierces the darkness once more. "Oh, Richie. I think that's very unlikely on a night like this, don't you? I'm not the betting kind, mind, but I imagine with no sign of your vehicle and the weather outside hurling cats and dogs, they'll all be safely tucked up in the station sipping coffee and eating donuts." Another guttural laugh fills the darkness. "Now Alby, he's the gambler, loves a game of cards. Got to play with a proper dealer once but didn't take to losing. Tied her to a chair and cut her over and over with the fine edge of a playing card. So many paper cuts. She cried and cried; she did. I reckon a bucket of the stuff. You should have been there, Richie; you would have liked it. You could have written one of your deaf metal songs about it."

Unable to hold back the fear any longer, Richie begins thrashing side to side, banging his already sore limbs against the walls of his cage and letting out a series of high-pitched cries. On the other side, her weight against the door, Margaret screams with him, matching his key and tone, clapping and stomping her feet to the rhythm of his fit.

"Inspiration, Richie," she says as they both finally settle. "One last song."

"I've got money. Not a lot, but—"

"Hush hush, dear. There's no need to be crude. Now, you must excuse me; I can't stand here all day tittle-tattling. There's work to be—"

"No, stay! Don't go!"

"Oh, Richie, you are a sweetie. All those tattoos and piercings, yet underneath all that, you're just a softie afraid of the dark, aren't you?"

"Please. Let's talk. We didn't really get a chance at dinner." *You crazy old bag.* "Tell me more about your adventures." *You saggy fucking trout.* It's all he's got, befriending the captor in the hope of striking a chord. He's seen it in the movies, probably the same ones she's seen.

"Saucepot, you with a girlfriend and all. You'll be asking me to take my teeth out next."

"No, seriously. The Amazon—was it hot?" *Was it hot? You stupid dumb fuck.*

"I'm flattered, but I must be going now."

"No, don't leave me alone, please."

"Oh, you're not alone, Richie; young Ezekiel's in there with you." She offers another throaty laugh. "What's left of him anyway." The screeching sound commences, and he knows as light fades, he's there for as long as they want him to be. "Rock 'n roll, Richie," Marge shouts, her subsequent laughter trailing off as the last of the light dies.

Left with only his own thoughts, Richie throws himself against the door. After several sob-fuelled and futile attempts, he finally creases into a corner, trying to get as far away as possible from the smooth round object he now knows to be young Ezekiel's bald head.

Melody

Melody feels dizzy and nauseous, her stomach twisting and turning like it's at war with itself. Her head swims and pounds like an army of marching drummers. *What the hell?* "Richie?"

She knows something is very off, but she can't piece it together, the fogginess lending the experience of a weekend break in Silent Hill. She squints, but everything remains blurry, the action only worsening her headache. "Richie? Richie!"

Nothing.

"The dinner," she mumbles. *It had to be the dinner!* It felt crazy to even think it, paranoia on steroids, but what other explanation was there for how bad she was feeling. *We were drugged. We were fucking drugged!* "Richie! Richie, where are you?!"

Silence.

No, not silence.

A shuffling from somewhere close as though something was dragging along the floor. It's faint, but it's there.

"Hello?"

The blurriness remains even as she blinks hard several times, distorted shadows within shadows. As her head continues its throbbing, approaching a crescendo of discomfort, she tries lifting her hand to her temple, but she can't move it. She tries again, yanking hard, her arms hardly moving as something cuts into her wrists.

Tied! I'm tied up. Why the fuck am I tied up?

The shuffle snaps her head to the right.

"Who's there?"

Only more shuffling, close.

"Hello?" She tries to move her legs, but they're bound too, tension biting into her ankles. "Is someone there?"

Silence.

Encouraged by the loosening of the string, she writhes some more against the softness beneath. But hope fades as something brushes against her right foot. Light, gentle, almost like *a feather?*

"Hello?"

As light pressure squeezes at her ankle, she inhales sharply and recoils, but the tension remains. Instinctively, thoughts turn to the old man, how he licked his lips and how his eyes almost ejected from his head as he ran them over her naked toes. She lets out a little cry and pulls back, but the pressure changes, becoming remarkably strong.

"Albert."

Through her blurred vision, she can see someone at the end of the bed, still wrapped in the fog. Nothing more than a silhouette, but she can see long bony fingers working at her feet, caressing them, massaging her arches.

"Why are you doing this?" she cries out, blinking manically to try and clear the fog. "Why?"

"Ooh-ooh ah-ah."

"Albert, please. You know this is wrong."

"Monkey see, monkey do."

"You're not a fucking monkey! You're a person. And this is—"

Her head snaps to the left, the shock factor delaying the sting that now sears across her cheek.

"I am a monkey. I am a monkey. Ooh-ooh ah-ah. Ooh-ooh ah-ah. I am a monkey. Say I'm a monkey. Say it!"

"Albert, you're *not* a monkey. You have to let—"

Her head snaps to the other side, the sting instantaneous this time. And as though the blow knocked more of the mist from her head, her vision becomes slightly clearer. Unconvinced that's a good thing, she studies the string wrapped tightly around her wrists and threaded through the far left headboard slat.

"Say it!"

"You're a monkey," she croaks, finally breaking into a sob. Driving her back against what she knows now to be a headboard—*Imagine what Zeke will think when our headboard is banging against those pink walls*—she instinctively tries bringing her legs into her chest, but Albert has a hold of her left foot and won't let go. She tries again to snap it away, but his cold bony fingers are coiled too tightly around the bone.

Relenting, she falls still, defeated and with tears running raw and unfiltered, snot running down her chin. She stares at the ceiling, eyes fixed on the materialising fan, trying her best to ignore the wetness between her toes as she counts the rotations. *Six. Seven. Eight. Nine. Make it stop!* Cold, oily, scaly, she feels his tongue expertly exploring the nooks and crannies in well-practised fashion. The old man moans and groans with pleasure as he drinks down her youth.

"Please, Albert. Please stop."

She feels the scrape of teeth as, one by one, her toes are sucked between thin crusty lips, the serpent within darting in and out excitedly. Her chest heaves as she cries without sound, eyes still fixed on the ceiling fan.

Thirty-one. Thirty-two. Thirty—

But as the old man bites down, she screams as if exorcising a demon from within—a primal, gut-wrenching shriek, the likes of which she's only ever heard in movies. She hears flesh giving, tearing, a fierce bolt of pain working through her as the old man's dentures cut into her skin. "Richieeeeeeeee!"

As vibrations of pain echo through her, remaining even as the pressure eases, she lets out a series of guttural rasps. Agony riddles her, exploring her in a way Albert did her toes, but searching well beyond.

"I am a monkey, aren't I?" Albert says between chews.

"Yes," she cries. "Yes."

"I like it when you scream. I like your eyes, too."

As the pain subsides a little, she tilts her head towards her chest, her vision clearing and allowing a view of the old man. Above the bulbous nose of broken blood vessels, his glossy eyes study her with hunger and childish excitement. Blood trickles from his wrinkled mouth and the fleshy substance between his lips that he continues to chew on like a child on toffee.

Melody starts to shake, feeling as though she's losing the plot. She and Richie watch this kind of thing on late-night TV, snacking on processed food and taking hits from the bong. All the cheesy horror movies they've watched, ridiculing and mocking the dumb protagonists. Not so fucking funny anymore.

And what if she manages to get away? Where is she going to go? The van's broken, and Richie has the keys anyway.

She closes her eyes on the verge of hysteria as Albert readies himself to bite down again. "Hey, Alby," she croaks, her voice shaking, the syllables scattered.

"What?"

"If you let me out, we can do other stuff. Perhaps we—" Melody swallows hard, praying to that imaginary god again—"We can add something else to that bucket list of yours."

Albert releases her foot, letting it fall back to the bed. "Dirty birdie! Dirty birdie!" Beating at his chest, he begins performing laps around the room.

Taking the opportunity, Melody surveys her surroundings, squirming into a less vulnerable position, convincing herself she'll kick out if Albert comes near her again. As the old nutter bellows like a monkey, beating at his skinny little chest, Melody watches, heart racing, all hope continuing to dwindle.

"I have to go," Albert finally says as he settles. "My teeth can't get through those bones of yours. Need my tools from the basement."

"No, Alby, please. You—you don't have to do this." She needs to buy time and find a way out of this mess. Perhaps if she can get the old loon close enough, she can strangle the fucker with her thighs; she's seen it done in the movies. "We can do something else. I bet I can do things that Marge can't."

Hunched over and smiling, Albert offers her a wink. "Dirty, dirty birdie."

"Please, Alby. Please."

"I won't be long," he promises, making his way out, stopping to turn a few feet away from the door. "If it helps, my dear, you are giving this fragile old man one of his dying wishes."

"Please."

"I'll say hi to your friend while I'm down there," the old man hollers, finally opening the door and exiting the room. She hears a small click, followed by his shuffling feet fading into the distance. Suddenly wishing she had someone to pray to, Melody starts to cry.

Chris

Something's holding him down. He can't feel his legs.

Inhale. Exhale. Inhale. Exhale.

Momentarily, he can't move, his mind showing images of the tree monster's lair, the pit of dirt, the twisting roots, and the earthy lid closing, forever sealing him underground. He lets out a scream, able to taste cheap scent and chemicals as he finally inhales.

Laundry powder.

His fingertips press into the softness beneath. *A mattress.* Someone put him into a bed and tucked him in tightly, too tightly. It's Grandma's house all over again: drenched in sweat, unable to escape the monster crawling towards him from the darkness, roots scraping across the wooden boards as it came for him. Even the smells are the same, a terrifying concoction of cheap wash powder, wood, and mould.

"Hey. Hey, let me out of here!"

He pushes against the blanket, but it's tight. So fucking tight and pressing against his gut. As he snaps his head left and right, he sees dim light beyond but no detail.

"Hey!"

His heart thunders against its cage as if as desperate to escape as he is. *Come on! Come on!* A grown man versus a sheet, and the sheet's winning. He feels weak, just like he did as a child, helpless as the monster creaked, groaned, and slaked its way towards him.

"Get me the fuck out of here!" He writhes against the starchy constraint, but it's as if a steel blanket pins him down. "Judy?"

Oh Christ, what the fuck?

"Judy!"

What have they done?

Inhale. Exhale.

Perhaps she's safe. Maybe she's in the car on the way to get help.

But he knows better. Judy didn't get away. She went down before he did; he saw it. She was a right mess. The crazy old fuckers must have given them something.

No way. No goddamn way.

He remembers now—their drinks and plates untouched. Why didn't that arouse suspicion? Because B&B generally doesn't stand for Bed & Bondage, he tells himself. He knew something was off from the get-go, though, but Judy wouldn't have it.

Fuck!

He thrashes and jerks, only succeeding in elevating his heart rate. *Come on!* But as if held by a supernatural force, the blanket hardly gives.

"I can't fucking breathe in here!"

Face getting redder by the minute, he tenses his arm muscles, trying to brute force his way from confinement, but his efforts are futile. "I hate these fucking blankets," he yells, slaking his hands across his chest and pushing with all his might. "Hate them. Hate them. Hate them."

Is this how he's meant to die? Perhaps all this time, those dreams were merely a twisted vision of his death. Not a monster after all, just a demon on his shoulder teasing with the knowledge of what was to come.

He begins a dampened cry, swallowing the gathering saliva and clawing at the sheet. He came here because he wanted to live, to experience life.

Stop giving up and get free; he scolds himself. *You want to live? Live. And Judy needs a fucking hero!*

He swallows hard, newly found determination coursing through his veins. Using his fingers like taloned claws, he scrapes them across the sheet, searching for a weak point, some give, anything. In his mind, he's digging his way through the dirt, trying to reach the surface. *Come on. Come on!* But hopes of it being a flimsy old threadbare blanket wane as his joints sing in agony, his fingers unable to find a way out or through the tightness.

"I—hate—these—fucking—BLANKETS!"

Instead of the dirt yielding, more of it collapses on top of him, pushing down on his chest, squeezing out the remaining air.

You want to live? Live. Live!

But in his mind, he hears more creaky groans of the tree monster. *You're not taking me!* He squirms and writhes his best he can, growling like a yard dog. He clenches his teeth, blood whooshing in his ears. Skin burns as it brushes across starchiness. His heart thumps wildly, making him think it might detonate at any moment.

Like the child at his grandma's house, he holds his breath, waiting to be drawn into oblivion.

But nothing.

And, after all this time, realisation finally dawns. And this is what it took.

It's him. He is the tree monster.

Throughout his youth, he was always looking for an escape, ways to outrun the monster. But he was only ever running from himself, running from roots, from his starchy parents, from anything that threatened his freedom. But then he fell in love, settled down, and only the pills and long hours at the office helped keep the *monster* at bay.

Judy!

This was his idea. A way of escaping the humdrum of retirement, to avoid pacing around within the four walls. Why couldn't he just embrace it? Be like Judy? *Because I'm just like Richie, running scared.*

"FUCK YOU!"

He suddenly feels like he owes his wife an apology. But first, he needs to get free, to raise the lid and climb from the dirt and moss, crawl through the mud of his own design and break free of the roots that have forever held him in place.

Adrenaline surges as he releases more throaty howls, thrashing as violently as his confines allow. As he snaps his head left to right and back again, he takes encouragement from the less limited movement, becoming even more manic as his hands manage to stretch the pink fabric further than before.

Movement. He hears movement.

"Judy, is that you?"

His finger joints continue their protests, but there is give. There is give! Biting at his lip, the taste of blood at the back of his throat, he thrusts upwards again, raising his arms undoubtedly higher than before. He takes the opportunity to look down, observing yet another sheet across his legs. *You've got to be fucking kidding.* But if he can work his upper half free, the rest will be easy. He'll be out. He'll be free!

More movement.

"Judy, hang on, I'm coming!"

He pushes again, roaring like the king of the fucking jungle they've found themselves in.

Welcome to the animal farm.

Panting hard, consumed by a need to escape, he continues working at the sheet, feeling himself emerging from the dirt pit. *I'm gonna get free of this, and then I'm going to find those old fuckers, and I'm going to kill them. I'm going to kill the shit out of them.*

It's working.

He lets out another roar, hearing his muscles tear and pop as he thrusts upwards with all his might. And finally, as the sheet loses all tautness, he pushes himself up, breaking the muddy surface, pushing past the mossy lid to put his head out into the freedom of the woods.

He takes a deep inhale of both worlds.

"Did you sleep well, Chris?" Marge asks from the side of the bed.

Oh fuck! He recoils, reaching down for the blanket across his legs, but Marge is already on him, swatting his aching efforts away with her shot-put arms. "No, please," he begs. "Please don't." But his efforts are weak, the needle plunging into his neck before he can raise his arm in defence.

"Please—"

There's just enough time to take in his surroundings before the blurriness begins taking effect: the familiar pink walls, the rolled out-pink tongue of a rug. But there's something different; the Jesus crosses are upside down, and the Lord's Prayer turned to face the wall.

As things begin to melt around him, he studies Marge's dripping old face, her crazy eyes staring over those bony cheeks exploding with clown-like blush. She looks positively gleeful, with gums the size of a dinner plate. "You've got some fight in you, Chris, I'll give you that. Are you having fun yet?"

Finally, she releases him, his head falling back into softness, his view of the ceiling fleeting as the sheet draws across him once more.

"I'll tuck you in nice and tight for your nap, Chris."

He tries to scream, tears working their way out of the corners of his eyes.

"Don't worry, Chris," the old woman's voice floats across in a slow-motion drawl. "I'm just having my fun until Alby is ready for you. This is all for him, after all. He's dying, you know, my poor sweet Alby. And I'm not going to let him go without doing what he's dreamt about. I'm sure you understand, what with you and your missus having your own bucket list and all. He's in with your wife right now, but he shouldn't be long."

Judy! My Judy!

Chris is already in another world, being dragged back down into the heart of the earth where the snaking vines torment him, the sticks and roots poking holes in his sides and wrapping themselves around his ribs.

As the tentacle-like limbs tickle his burning lungs, mocking his revelation, he decides this was his fate after all.

The lid comes down again.

Judy

Judy groans as she comes to, an impossibly loud beat drumming in her head. Her vision is blurry and grainy, but from what she can tell, the ground beneath appears to be spinning. She tries to move, but her limbs flare with pain, a searing tormenting agony as if someone is exploring her rawness with a red-hot poker. Down her left side, too, a slightly duller ache, but catching up fast.

The gag across her mouth catches her scream.

She studies her wrists, bound to the hanging chains by black tape, likely the same that seals her mouth shut. Pressure on her ankles tells her that her legs are also tied up.

Oh, please God, no.

And as realisation hits that it's her spinning and not the ground, she lets out a series of muffled screams, knowing Chris was right, that there's something very wrong with their hosts.

She scolds herself, imagining slapping herself on the wrist as the old lady did on their first encounter. How many red flags did she need, for Christ's sake? The mysterious Beatrice, the self-flagellation, the preening, and the dancing chimp routine. But nobody would expect to wake up from an overnight stay in a country guesthouse suspended from the ceiling, even it had a one-star rating. And she's never read anything on Yelp about this.

She sobs, liquid from her eyes, nose, and mouth spilling to the floor.

I'm so sorry, Chris. She tries to imagine him by her side, which helps a little. She sucks in some air, grimacing as her limbs continue to scream. *What do I do, love? What do I do?*

Swear jar out the window; this is one hell of a fucking mess, she considers. *Fuck, fuck, fuckity-fuck.*

Something in the food, the food *they* didn't touch. Or the wine, perhaps.

She tries to blink past the headache, squinting to try and bring clarity to her surroundings, but it's like looking through murky water. Across the way, she thinks she makes out the outline of a door. Beneath her, what looks like cracked and discoloured concrete continues spinning. She swings herself around, managing to steal a glance immediately to her right. Lit by a morsel of blurry light from a single cracked bulb screwed into the wall, there's a giant oil burner, pixelated metal tentacles snaking out and reaching up towards the ceiling. The basement, perhaps. Maybe Chris and the others are down here as well, she considers.

Okay, think, Judy. Think!

If she can somehow free herself, she can find the car and get help. But she starts second-guessing herself, thinking the door is likely locked and the car is no longer there. The old couple might look as gormless as goldfish, but she feels this isn't their first rodeo—all that weird talk last night of bucket lists and *games.* At the very least, they would have taken the car keys from Chris, surely? And she doesn't even entertain the thought of Chris having somehow escaped and on the way to get help. Those kinds of thoughts are dangerous. *And this isn't the movies.*

First things first, though, how does she get herself down?

Judy starts jiggling as much as she can, the sound of what she assumes to be several chains above grating on her soul, but she persists. Perhaps if she can build enough momentum, the whole thing will come crashing down, and she can make her escape. The pain in her side makes itself known, overtaking the burning in her arms and legs.

Come on, Judy!

Chains above moan and creak as they tangle, bringing her closer to a full circle each time. Gritting her teeth, letting out more muffled groans, she leans as best she can, momentarily getting a flashback of rusty and damp childhood playgrounds.

It's working.

She can make out a crack in the floor and some boxes on the shelf to her left. Chains creaking and moaning, she swings back around and past the boiler, noting some tools hanging on the wall.

Come on!

And back again, chains screaming along with her. And again. *Creak. Creak.* And again. *Creak.* Until she can make out another door and a freezer on the far left wall. And now a—

Shoe.

The scream is mostly internal, only a slightly muted cry escaping from her taped mouth. Helplessly, she spins back around, flailing her arms, but only managing to brush a finger across Alby's waiting and smiling face.

"You're my favourite," he says, grabbing a handful of her hair and bringing her close.

She can see every purple vein on his nose, every hair sprouting from the cavernous nostrils. And the yellowing damp, watery eyes that she considers clawing out.

"I hope you play nice, Judy. If not, I have tools to help," he says, peeling back the tape across her mouth.

In the old man's other hand, pinched between withered and bony fingers, she spies a Tupperware container with a bright pink lid.

"What—what's in that?" she asks, mind racing, knowing it unlikely to be homemade biscuits.

Albert's face lights up like a boy running towards a mountain of gifts on Christmas morning.

"Don't worry," he says gleefully, shaking the box in front of her face. "Just took a little slice off your side. Got my pound of flesh."

"What? What are you talking about?" She searches his face looking for a flicker of jest, but the bolt of pain near her left hip is the only answer she needs. Her first instinct is to yell, scream and hit out, but she's already caught a glimpse of the rusty tools hanging on the wall. "Why—why would you?"

"Margie took real good care of the wound, don't worry."

She recalls the conversation from the dinner table. *I was a nurse, and Albert was a journalist, see.*

"It won't get infected or anything," Albert continues. "We learned a long time ago how to take someone apart slowly and keep them alive. Fresh is best."

"You cut a piece out of me?" *You cut a piece out of me. You cut a piece out of me.*

"Just a slice." Albert's gummy smile grows wider, adding to her nausea and dizziness. And the pain lancing her side, all the more real now, making her feel she might vomit. Part of her wishes for it to happen, a spray of gunk to fire all over the old bastard's head. It would serve the fucker right.

"I'm gonna cook it later," he says with a smile. "Can cook up a storm, I can."

The thought prompts another dry gag.

"I might even let you have a bit," Albert says, following with a loud snort. "Oh, my Margie. She ain't perfect, but she's a good girl, loves me like nothing else. I'm sick, see. Don't have much time, so she's come out of retirement to help me tick the last few things off the list."

It's like a nightmare, only the pain is too real, and the initial blurriness has given way to terrifying clarity. But things like this don't happen to folk like them. That's not the way the cookie's supposed to crumble.

"Cat got your tongue, Judy?" Albert says, bringing her closer, his nose hair tickling her cheek as he inhales. "I hope not. That's the best bit."

Her level of anger surprises her, as though fear should be taking up all the room. But she's furious, livid. If she could only break free and get her hands on the brittle little fucker, God only knows what she'd do. Sunday Service might no longer be an option, but she's already at peace with that.

The old man inhales again. "Sweet, sweet, meat."

"Please let me go, Albert."

"I don't know what you're talking about. This place is lovely and airy; it's not like we've trapped you under the stairs or anything."

She's always the level-headed one, the voice of reason with a butter wouldn't melt attitude. But this is something else, tapping into a part of her that nothing else ever has. Before she can talk herself out of it, she looks him in the eyes and spits in the one pointing right, taking some pleasure in the frothiness leaking down his leathery face.

Albert wipes his free spindly arm across his cheek, his smile gone. "Now that wasn't very lady-like," he says in a wounded puppy kind of way. "I thought you were the nice one, but now I'm not so sure."

"You fucking sicko," Judy cries. "You lousy chimp-gimp sack of fucking bones." The pain subsides as anger takes over, the chains rattling above, but Albert keeping hold. "You know what you are?" she says, hardly able to believe *that* word is going to leave her lips. "You're a monkey's cunt is what you are."

Albert inhales sharply, the hairs in his nostril rustling in the wind. "Oh my, oh my," he says, dragging his skinny arm across his face. "Meany meany fish and taty! That other lady is much nicer than you," he says, as though this declaration is meant to offend. "A bit of a dirty birdie, mind you, but she never spat in my eye. Would if I asked her to, I expect." He finally lets Judy go, sending her spinning as he works his way around, reaching for the knife and heavy-duty saw.

"Where's my husband? Where's Chris?"

"Only came down here for this; didn't expect you to be awake already. You've made me all sad, and now I'm going to tell Margie."

"I said, where's Chris?"

Tools in hand, Albert grabs her by the neck and smooths the tape back in place. He brings her in close and runs a tongue up the side of her face. "You taste bitter," he says.

Judy cringes, the tape pulling at her skin. Unable to look Albert in the eye, her gaze finds the forest of grey protruding from the man's ear and the black bug hovering nearby. She watches it disappear somewhere within, and as Albert instinctively digs a bony translucent finger into the canal, audibly crushing the insect and dragging it across his cheek, creating a sideburn of bug guts. What's left on his finger, he sucks between his crispy lips. "Ooh-oh, ah-ah."

Speckling her gag with bile, Judy quickly swallows the rest so as not to choke, grimacing at the burn in her throat and sour taste going down.

Finally, Albert releases his bony grip, sending Judy spinning and the chains screaming, echoing her pain. She catches glimpses of Albert making his way towards the closed door, tools in one hand and Tupperware box in the other.

"Where's Chris?" she cries, wincing at the stale taste vomit.

But Albert turns, no smile this time. "How would I know? I'm just a monkey's cunt."

She hears the door close but doesn't see it, no wiser to where it leads. Heart thundering, she takes long, deep breaths to try and remain calm. She has some time; He'll be gone for a while, preoccupied with whatever he's going to do with the saw. Trying to blank out such thoughts, she knows she can't waste a second. No time to worry for her husband either, however harsh that sounds, but she knows such a distraction would be a guaranteed death sentence for them both. She needs her wits, her sharpness.

She grits her teeth and tilts her head back, looking for an ounce of hope. But the bolt holding the chains looks brand new, with no wear or tear, no chance of a rusty fixing popping out and setting her down.

Think, Judy. MacGyver this fucker! Like the original, not that crappy reboot, either. Be like Hannibal with a random garage, five minutes, and the A-Team van.

But do fucking something, Judy!

For the love of God, do something.

But the tape is bound tightly around her wrists with no give at all to try and work herself free. Eyes on the walls of tools, she tries her best to sway towards it, but each time falls at least a foot short. She focuses on the tape around her mouth, knowing even if she could work it free, she wouldn't be able to bring her wrists close enough to bite through. But it's a start, something to distract.

I will get out of here.

Judy starts to channel that college version of herself, gritting her teeth behind the tugging tape. Morbid Angel's song, *Ageless, Still I Am*, thrashes in her mind.

—5—

The Great Escape

The clock's ticking.

As she continues throwing herself around on the bed, the thought of Albert returning with his *tools* curdles Melody's blood. Some of it already stains the pink sheets, turning her stomach further. Pain ripples through her with every jerk and twist, but she refuses to go down like this.

Come the fuck on!

She focuses on her legs, having wasted too much time futilely trying to work her hands free. She's getting somewhere, too. Looking at the half-assed attempts at knots, she figures the old man's brittle hands likely got tired working the rope around them. It's working. *I'm gonna fuck you up old man!* Brave talk, she figures, that's all, as her head now fills with thoughts of reuniting with Richie.

Come on, Melody! Now's the time to get fucking metal!

If she can somehow make it to the chest of drawers on the other side of the room, maybe there'll be a knife, scissors, something to work through the rope around her wrists. *Then I'll slit that old turkey's giblet of a throat. Maybe.*

A little bit of extra flexibility with every squirm encourages her to continue thrashing away, her limbs screaming for a rest, her breathing fast and erratic. Part of her regrets not kicking the old man in the head, but at the same time, knowing he likely would have killed her for it. At least this way, she has a fighting chance. She thinks of the night at Richie's show when some chick said she wasn't *death* enough to be there. Bitch called her a poser, and Melody showed her just how metal she could be. In her mind now, she can hear the crowd chanting, "Fight! Fight! Fight! Fight!" That's who I am, she tells herself. That's who the fuck I am.

Something gives. She's out. At least her legs are.

No way. No fucking way. I did it!

Melody grimaces, swinging her legs to the carpet, the pain obligingly overwhelming and almost bringing her down as she puts pressure on her chewed toes. Riding it out, she pokes her nose through the drawn pink curtains, observing the dimly lit driveway below, judging it too far down to jump.

Richie, I don't wanna die.

Not dwelling on it, she begins pulling at the bed, only managing to budge it half an inch with every yank, the thick pink shag working against her. If it were a double bed, she'd be fucked, she figures. *Bless you, Beatrice, whoever and wherever you are, you lovely little prude.*

A moment of clarity for Melody dictates if she and Richie make it out alive, they will find a nice little corner of suburbia. Nothing too flashy: two bedrooms, maybe three, depending on how good a number she can do on her fiancé. A nice big shed for when Richie's mates come round to practice.

Lovely little herb garden for her, one of her lesser well-known desires. And not a bloody carpet in sight, not even a fucking welcome mat at the door.

She pulls again, pain echoing through her, the carpet's fabric tickling the rawness of her toe's torn meat and exposed bone. She refuses to quit, tears in her eyes and streaks of black makeup running down her cheeks.

Again.

And again.

And again.

Each time she pulls, the string burns more, feeling like it might just slice through her wrists. Might still be a better way to go, she thinks. She swallows hard, knowing she'll never holiday in the countryside again, complimentary breakfast or not.

She hears voices. *Where are they coming from? How far?*

Holding her breath, she tracks the muffled noise to somewhere below.

I can do this. I can do this.

Teeth cutting into her lip, veins in her arms like twisted tree roots, Melody heaves with all her might. She turns her head towards the chest of drawers that still seems so far away, but on sight of the stack of envelopes, notepad, and more importantly, the letter opener with the old-fashioned-looking handle, she gets a second wind, a surge of adrenaline. Offering dampened groans, she drags the wooden bed slowly across the floor, leg muscles tightening against the resistance and sending extra twinges of pain. Carpet continues to infiltrate the open wounds in her toes, fibres sticking to the bloody mess and becoming one. She grits her teeth through the tears, occasionally offering a quiet but hysterical laugh that scares her further. *It's a new feeling, Richie, something I've never experienced, indescribable.* Purely as a distraction, she begins playing one of his songs in her head.

You think you're evil, but you've got to learn
Lend me your ears, and I'll make them burn
You ain't seen nothing yet, fucker!

Cos' I'm gonna make your asshole—She pauses, holding her breath as the voices stop—*pucker.*

In preparation for hearing the staircase's creak, Melody screws her eyes half shut, chewing at her lip. *Shit! Shit! Shit!* Momentarily, she convinces herself she can hear soft wooden moans, but a bout of hacking brings relief. What was it the old man said about him dying? *Not fucking soon enough.*

As the muffled conversation picks up again, Melody continues her mission, blood pounding in her head, pain secondary but never far away.

Come on! Come on!

Five feet to go, if that. The crowd chants, "Fight! Fight! Fight! Fight!"

Even if she manages to get hold of the letter-opener, Melody begins to wonder if she'll be able to cut through the string. But first things first, she has to make it there; besides, it works in the fucking movies, and they gotta base that shit on something.

To the sound of more rasping, she continues dragging the bed across until, if her hands weren't bound, she'd be within touching distance. She sucks in some air, allowing her limbs a brief reprieve.

Three.

Two.

One.

With another hard yank, Melody positions herself as close to the chest of drawers as possible, her side painfully coming up against its edge. She doubles over and grasps the antique letter-opener between her teeth. With no time to celebrate small victories, she hunches over as far as her body allows, opening up her right palm, and observing the cuts across her wrists. She can't afford to miss; every second counts. Otherwise, it's hello Alby, goodbye toes.

Finally, she opens her mouth to release the letter-opener, coiling her fingers around the handle as it lands safely in her palm. Maybe there is a God, she thinks.

I fucking made it here! I fucking did it! Wait until I tell Richie about this. I just have to cut this rope, and I'll go find him. We'll leave this fucking place together and—

The thought brings a wave of fresh tears, but she blinks them away, refusing to give the saggy, cross-eyed fucker any more of her than he's already taken. Once more, she prays to whoever might be listening as she begins clumsily working the blade across the string, always listening for the sound of creaking stairs. She knows it's coming. What if she gets free? What next? She recalls Albert's parting words from before, "*I'll* say hi to your friend while I'm down there." *Did he mean Richie? If they fucking hurt him –*

The sight of the frayed string has her working the blade across with further intensity. Chewing at the inside of her lip, she settles into a rhythm, encouraged as more fine strands become errant from the pack.

Come on! Come on!

She can hardly believe it as the string falls to the blood-stained carpet. But just as she lunges for the door, the stairs creak.

Melody freezes, sucking in her breath. Feeling as though her stomach has just dropped out, she searches the room, her grip tightening further on the letter-opener. Could she? Would she? Absofucking-lutely if that's what it came down to. She holds onto her breath, listening to every terror-inducing groan, the fogginess in her head well and truly dissipated.

The voices get closer, but the conversation is still incoherent.

She tenses, prepared to spring.

Creak.

She can feel her arm trembling as she lifts the weapon over her shoulder. Oh Jesus! Jesus fucking Christ!

Creak.

Pinning herself against the wall near the door, she gets ready to strike, trying to convince herself she has the guts to do it.

Creak.

She visualises bringing the blade down into the old man's neck, his jugular spurting like the *crimson flow of the devil's orgasm*—more of Richie's lyrics. But what of Marge? What good will the tiny blade serve against a woman of such epic proportions? She likens it to trying to bring a bull down with a knitting needle.

Creak.

She swallows the lump that forms in her throat; the slowness of their approach makes it all the more terrifying. Dying or not, she can't afford to underestimate their abilities or the sheer evil of the World's Greatest Grandma and sidekick. Her eyes flick to the weapon in her blood-greased palm.

Creak.

I can do this. I can do this. I can do this.

Melody continues the chant, only half-believing her words. She's done some bad things in her time, including a bit of theft and burglary, but she's never stabbed a grandpa in the neck. That was never on her bucket list.

Fuck this fucking place! But do it cos you've never done it. Right, Richie?

Creak.

Shit.

She overhears part of their conversation, something about not having enough tape.

Another cough. Another creak.

So close. Her fingers curl around the handle of the blade.

She hears Marge mention Judy's name, the rest of the sentence nothing but a raspy mess.

Creak.

They're on the landing. *Oh shit! Oh shit!* She hears them shuffling towards her, more muted conversation, and the occasional snigger. They draw closer, Melody's fingers aching, her jaw sore from clenching.

"Is it everything you hoped for?" she hears Marge say with far too much clarity for her liking.

"And more, dear," Albert replies. "I'm one happy monkey."

"Love you, Alby."

"Love you, Marge."

And the shuffling stops.

Melody inhales sharply, suddenly feeling as weak as a kitten.

I don't want to die. I don't want to die. I'm sorry for everything I've done, but please don't let me die.

As the key rattles in the door, she holds her breath and grips her weapon so tightly that her hand begins to cramp.

"No, wait," Albert says from behind the door. "She's my new favourite. Let's do her last."

"Oh, Alby, just like your Yorkshire Puddings, always saving the best for last."

"Sprouts first. Bleurgh!"

"I'll always be your true favourite, though, won't I, Alby?"

"Of course you will, Margie. Hey, do you remember that night we made love in that trucker's blood, underneath the stars?"

"Remember? Between your jumpy monkey sex and the concrete pushing on my old hips, I could hardly walk for days. Beautiful night though. I can still smell the copper in the air."

"I felt like King Kong that night," Albert says, punctuated with another hacky explosion of coughing.

Melody lets her breath go, listening to their feet retreating down the corridor.

"—always be my King Kong, love."

She puts her ear to the door, following the continued soft creaking until it stops a little further left. There's another click, and the shuffling grows distant. Sounds like they've entered another room, Melody figures.

Now. It has to be now.

Screwing her eyes half-closed, Melody turns the door handle. Locked. Fuck it to Hell and back. She crouches, hoping for her misspent youth to pay off as she carefully threads the blade through the hole. With her face still creased, she quietly goes to work, half-expecting the door to be flung open against her head.

Come on! Come on! Click, damn you.

She hears dampened moans. A man. *Richie?*

And what if she does manage to get the door open? She has three choices, she figures: make a run for it and pray she can get out, try to sneak past and avoid any confrontation, or enter the room swiping with the letter opener. She'll figure it out if she gets that far.

Come on! Come the fuck on!

But her shaking fingers won't relent.

—6—

The Great Escape
Second Leg

"**W**akey wakey, rise and shine," Marge sings. "The day is wasting!"

Head pulsating, Chris tries to rise, but the goddamn lid is back on tight.

"Not yet, Albert."

Albert nods submissively, taking a step back and placing the saw on the bedside table next to the small portable cooking stove they usually keep in the camper-van. "Sorry. Just excited."

"I know, dear," Marge says, working her hands down the side of the bed. "But softly, softly, catchee monkey."

The entire ordeal begins flashing through Chris' mind, a nightmare on steroids, the old people grinning and the tree monster groaning. But the fabric pinning him down is as real as is the stench of laundry powder and cough lozenges. Something else, too. Burning? And the shapes moving beyond the stretched blanket, not figments of the imagination, not spindly tree limbs, but bona fide fucking monsters, and only the Devil knows what they're capable of.

"Right, let's get you out of these sheets and cook you a nice breakfast, shall we?" Marge croaks, huffing and puffing as she continues tugging at the blanket. "My, I did a proper number this time, didn't I?"

Chris studies Marge's blurry and pudgy face as the blanket rips away, thinking she looks like a psychotic magician pulling off the greatest trick of the century. He half expects her to take a bow, gracing him with another glance at the knobbly mess sitting atop her scalp and those enormous shrivelled dangly breasts.

"There he is," Marge says. "Did you sleep well, Chris? Sweet dreams, I hope."

Chris looks at the clock to see it's only just past midnight. "Where's Judy?" he slurs, trying to push himself up and drag free from the second blanket wrapped just as tightly around his midriff. "What have—have you done with her?"

"She's just hanging around downstairs," Albert says jovially. "Snug as a bug in a rug."

What the fuck does that mean? With a wild moan, Chris tries again to push himself to his elbows, but his arms continue to fail him. "What the fuck have you done to Judy?" There's little feeling in them and even less beneath his waist. *The blanket—too tight. Can't feel—*

"Easy, Chris," Marge says. "You've likely got one hell of a hangover."

"You drugged us. Something in the—" Chris' eyes widen as he turns his head, tracking the crackling sound to his right. A million thoughts rush through his head as he studies the orange glow of the stove, the serrated knife, and the rusty saw sitting next to it. "What are—what's that for?"

"Breakfast in Bed, Chris." Marge rubs her hands. "Ready, dear?"

"Ready, Margie."

Chris watches as Albert picks up the knife, the old man's watery eyes oozing excitement. "The fuck are you going to do?" he says, trying again to push himself up, his body refusing to listen, basking in drugged lethargy.

"You have to understand; this is nothing personal, Chris. This is just our swan song, so to speak. Alby's last supper."

"Don't. Don't do this."

"There, there, Chris," Marge says, enveloping his forehead with one of her big hands. "You'll feel nothing but a pinch."

With Albert hovering over him, wielding the blade, and the stove crackling its readiness, Chris tries to scream, but his mouth is as dry as a flour mill. He tries again to get up, this time making it to his elbows. "Margaret, please." He watches her working around the bottom blanket, ready for her next magic trick. "Albert, you don't need to do this."

"But I'm starving," the old man replies. "What did your friend say about eating a tramp's head?"

And with one dramatic swoop, Margaret whips the bottom blanket away.

Again, Chris tries to conjure a scream, but only a dry rasp emerges. Momentarily, he convinces himself his eyes are playing tricks, that he's lost in dreamland again where the trees come alive, and that soon He'll wake up, shaken but with no monsters to be seen. Judy will be beside him, doing her crossword. "Don't let your cocoa get cold, dear."

Because this can't be real, this can't be happening.

"Surprise!" Margie sings.

As the room begins to rotate, Chris grips the sheet underneath, holding on for dear life. Willing himself not to pass out, knowing this could be the end times, his stare remains fixed on the rounded stub where his right leg should be, the centre of gravity for the shades of pink that spin around it. "Where's my fucking leg?" he asks, a question he never thought would leave his lips.

"Downstairs in the oven," Marge replies, offering Albert a nod. "It's soaking in a nice marinade of beer and mustard oil. We picked that little nugget up on a little trip to India—almost tested it there and then on one of the locals, but we honoured our pledge to wait."

"I'm starving," Albert repeats, readying himself with the knife, a stream of drool dangling from his thin, cracked lips.

Margaret shuffles around to Albert's side, giving her hands a rub as she looks down at Chris. "This is just a little starter to keep him going before the main course."

"Stay the fuck away," Chris cries, veins popping in his neck as he tries to force his body awake. "Stay the fuck away from me!"

But helplessly, he watches as Albert places a bony hand at the top of his left thigh and begins running the blade across his leg. Nothing but a *pinch*. At first sight of magnificent red, Chris starts shaking his head, growling, spitting, praying for his useless remaining limbs to work.

"You fucking fucks!!"

He bites down hard, puncturing his lip, the sensation of pain much stronger than that emanating from his thigh, where the blood begins to pool on either side. He lashes out with his arms, falling back to the bed again, the sounds of the blade chewing his flesh and grinding his bones filling his ears. Finally, he finds a scream, a blood-curdling cry of realisation that *he's* the breakfast in bed. "Please, stop! Please!"

"Got it," Albert says, holding the bloody mess out in front, looking proud as punch as though he's just removed a tumour from a dying patient. "Fresh is best. Fresh is best," he says excitedly. That same squirrely tongue that molested Melody's toes snakes out of those drooling lips to lick the blood dripping from the slab of meat.

As the sizzling begins, Chris snaps his head to the left, trying to get as far away from the sound of his cooking flesh as possible. "You're fucking mad," Chris cries. "I'll fucking kill you. I'll fucking kill you!" But rage quickly turns to sobbing, grim reality wrapping around him like a *heavy blanket*, that he's likely going to die in this musty fucking place, so many things on his bucket list left unchecked.

The smell instantly nauseates, already settling at the back of his throat. It's one he knows would stay with him for the rest of his days in the unlikely event of making it out alive. *I'm sorry, Judy. I'm so very sorry.*

"We're not so different, Chris," Marge says. "Born with a yearning to be unique, not just a pawn in this crazy fucking life. Alby didn't want a dog, and I didn't want to be in the kitchen all day cooking taters and veg. Peas in a pod, if you like, with a fascination for the dark side. We made a list of things we wanted to do before we died. Our marriage vows, so to speak."

"Oh, I almost forgot," Alby says, swivelling around. He snatches the Tupperware box from the windowsill and prises off the lid, spilling contents onto the griddle. "I wonder if your wife will taste sweeter?"

"You're fucking savages! You fucking—" Chris wills himself to get up, but his muscles protest, nothing more than aching sacks of jelly. He studies his missing leg again, still unable to accept it's gone. A momentary thought fills his head that this is all some sort of sick fucking joke. That a camera crew may jump out from behind the curtains any moment to tell him he's been part of some new prank show. But hope can play strange tricks on the mind. "You fucking fuuuuuuucks!"

"We saw a lot of it out there on our travels, didn't we, Alby? All sorts of wonders and grotesque savagery. But the biggest taboo, the one we saved until last—"

"Like the puddings," Albert cries, excitedly drumming his arms against his side. "Like the puddings."

"Yes, like the puddings, dear. Because we wanted something to look forward to, something to keep us going through the downtimes."

"You're nothing but bones and batshit crazy."

"And when Alby got his cancer diagnosis—"

"It meant it was time for pudding," Albert cries. "Human pudding!"

"Don't forget to turn the meat, Alby," Marge says, giving him an elbow. "You don't want it to burn."

"Oh, yeah."

"What about your kids? Your grandkids?" Chris says, trying to ignore the heightened sizzling as he reaches for a connection, something to help put an end to the madness. "All the family you said you had around here. Think of what it would do to them when all this catches up with you."

"Your concern means the world, but it's all rather unnecessary," Margaret says, taking the knife from Albert and running her tongue along the blade to collect the blood. "See, we have no family. It's just Alby and me, always has been, ever since we were old enough to escape our living Hell."

"You're not human," Chris says, realising he's wasting his breath. "Whatever your story, this—this is not right!"

"I'm not waiting any longer," Albert says, hovering his fingers over the stove. "Hmm, I've forgotten which one's which now. Chris or Judy. Chris or Judy. Eeny meeny." He grabs one of the slices of meat with his bony digits and brings it towards his dry lips. "Damn, it's hot." He begins hopping from foot to foot, spraying spittle across the cut of meat as he tries to blow it cool.

With thoughts racing through his head, none of them rational, Chris helplessly watches the old man blowing on the fleshy chunk. As anger momentarily overrides terror, he lunges, intending to claim it, but instead, his arms fail him, his face finding the softness of the mattress.

"He's right," Margaret says, slapping her dying husband on the back of his head. "Guests first." She hands the knife to Albert, approaches the bed, and roughly grabs Chris by the hair, forcefully bringing his head back. Knowing what's coming, Chris flails his arms, but his weak limbs redundantly glance off her chunkiness. He clamps his jaw tightly shut, but the burly woman efficiently manages to drive two fingers between his lips. And before he can bite down, her big hands are working into his mouth, prising it open and forcing a series of gags. "Alby!"

"But this is mine," Albert says, holding the flesh to his chest like a teddy bear.

"Plenty to go around," Margaret says. "Just trim off a little slice."

The old man sighs and uses the knife to carve off a mouthful. He picks it up between his misshapen fingers. "Chu-chu," he says before cramming the meat into Chris' mouth. Chris instinctively tries to spit it out, but Margaret clamps his jaw shut again and slips a hand across his lips.

"It's good," the old man says, biting into the glistening darkness. "But I want to try the heart next or the liver, something different."

"As long as you don't spoil your appetite, Alby. There's a joint in the oven, don't forget."

"So can I?"

"At least finish what you have in your hand first, you greedy little monkey."

"Ooh-oh ah-ah."

As Chris tries to escape Marge's grip, doing all he can to avoid swallowing what could very well be a medium-rare slice of his wife, he hears a creak and spies a tuft of dark hair near the bottom of the doorframe. He continues his struggles, the possibility of being rescued from the ordeal offering renewed hope. The eyes come into view, wide and manic. It's the young lady—Melody? As a means of communication, a desperate plea, he widens his own eyes and offers an elevated series of groans, thrashing as much as his semi-conscious body will allow.

"Give me a hand, Alby, will you?" Marge says, "Our guest is getting a bit lively."

And as Albert joins Margaret in restraining him, Chris watches Melody make her run, unconsciously swallowing his complimentary breakfast.

***

Fuck! Fuck! Fuck! Fuck! And fuck!

Guilt gnawing at her, Melody grips the banister, legs threatening to buckle any moment and pain echoing. She carefully straddles the rail and begins a slow descent, squeezing the wood with her hands to avoid going down too quickly, grimacing as it gives off a faint squeak. Still better than taking her chances down the stairs, she figures, already witnessing their terrifying groans.

As she arrives near the bottom, her ankle catches on a large metal shelving unit, creating a sharp clang. She holds onto her cry and grips down hard on the railing, expecting the shuffling to commence any second.

But nothing from above, only a soft thudding coming from somewhere close.

From the unit.

Chewing on the inside of her mouth, she waits it out, still sure as hell she'll soon see the odd couples' wizened faces peering over the top of the staircase, wondering what the loud noise was. She imagines the old man holding the saw and knife above his head, the blood of the retired accountant smeared across his cheeks like warpaint. And Marge following behind, the stove in her right hand, crackling and fizzing away. Suddenly, the thudding seems impossibly loud, adding to the likelihood of her vision coming true.

To try and distract herself, Melody focuses her attention on the grandfather clock and the hypnotic swing of the pendulum. The clock's inevitable age and stateliness lend her the feeling of being a child again, vulnerable and afraid, wary of her elders.

Tick-tock. Tick-tock. Tick-tock.

Only to the sound of Albert's chimp impressions does she finally lower herself to the bottom, placing her head against the wall next to the shelf. She feels the vibrations and hears the gentle clanking of the heavy-looking unit.

"Richie?" she whispers, knowing her voice unlikely to carry through. "Richie," she mutters again hopefully.

From above there's a long, drawn-out wail that makes her skin prickle and twists her stomach. Telling herself there's nothing she can do; she coils her fingers around the side of the metal unit and heaves, its coarse edges immediately cutting into her skin. She tries from the other side, using her body weight to slide it across, but her skinny frame can't budge it an inch. She imagines him trapped in there, wedged in the darkness. Knowing all that he's been through adds to the intense pressure as she searches frantically—*for what?* A fucking forklift?

Shit. Shit. Shit.

Her mind won't stop reminding her that through the lounge is the kitchen diner. And the front door.

I can't leave him. Not my Richie.

She tries again, throwing herself against the unit, but it stubbornly remains in place.

Above, there are more pained cries from Chris and a series of gentle thuds on the ceiling, Albert no doubt performing his chimp dance once more. Knowing the grandfather clock's ticking, she begins searching for her phone, starting in the lounge and working through to the kitchen, grabbing a silver knife from the cutlery drawer, her search, otherwise proving fruitless. The oven whirs in the background, but she has no intention of checking how *the joint is* doing.

We don't even have a phone, so intrusive I find them.

Fuck!

Melody coils her fingers tightly around the knife, weighing up her chances against the old fuckers upstairs. Two against one, but she has youth on her side.

Marge has a bit of a weight advantage, though, Melody!

She can't shake the image of Chris, his missing leg, the saw, and the bloody meat hanging from Albert's mouth. Most of all, the look on the poor man's face as she made eye contact. But what scared her even more was the look on Albert and Margaret's faces: wild, inhuman, and beyond animalistic. *Savage.*

And besides, yes, she's stolen a credit card or two in her time, even hot-wired a car in her teenage years, but going up against two psychopaths with a taste for torture is a whole new ballgame. And the state of him by now, he's likely already dying. She would be too late.

Yeah, just keep telling yourself that, you chickenshit.

Eyes on the dark rippling puddles outside partially lit by the light spilling from the kitchen, her instincts scream at her to open the front door and run like the wind. She can get help, find the closest neighbour, use the phone, and call the police. Which direction, though? And how far? It's pitch black, and the van's fucked. No sign of the other car that was parked down the driveway last night.

A gust of wind wraps around the building, sending the rain pounding against the glass.

Fuck this! Fuck this!

Regardless, she grabs the door handle, her stomach twisting, blood pounding in her head. *I'll come back for you, Richie.* But just as she begins twisting it, she hears the faintest of screams, this one different from the fading ones upstairs and unmistakably female.

Oh, come on!

Thinking there's every chance she's going to end up like all the other protagonists in those ever-so predictable but binge-worthy, bong-worthy movies, the sound of another scream prompts her to release the handle. *Am I really? Am I really going to fucking do this?* Knowing it must be Judy, she figures both of them might be able to move the unit, and then they can all—well, the majority of them— make their escape from this fucking nuthouse.

Back in the lounge, her skin prickles at the sound of more blood-curdling howls upstairs. No doubt that the cries are getting weaker, which means her time is limited. Dust sprinkles from the ceiling to the sound of more faint chimp impressions, Albert likely spoiling his appetite for dinner.

That scream again. *Somewhere below.* Coming from—

Of course this fucking hell house has a basement. Eyes on the door in the far wall, she waits for the crystals on the ceiling light to begin their jiggle before finally making her run, not wanting to spend a moment longer than necessary in this horror house. She turns the handle, expecting it to be locked, coolness blasting her as she takes the first step into darkness.

"Who's there?" a woman's voice croaks.

Recognising it as Judy's, Melody closes the door behind her and makes her way carefully down the concrete steps. "It's Melody."

"Oh, thank Christ! Thank goodness."

"Shh. We have to be quiet."

"Get me down. I can't bear it anymore."

As the weak, cracked orange light lends further unpleasant grittiness to the scene of Judy hanging from the ceiling by chains, hands bound by tape, Melody jumps the remaining two steps and rushes across. She starts with Judy's wrists, expecting the door to fly open any moment.

"Hurry," Judy says.

"I'm trying." She works the knife into the knotted mess—*this ain't no Christmas wrapping*—trying futilely to work through the tape. "Fuck!"

"Please just hurry," Judy cries.

"I am. I am." The tape twists and turns as Melody continues working at it, hoping she may be able to fray the edges enough to rip through it. *Come on. Come on.*

Wincing as her wrists sing out, Judy half-screws her eyes shut, noting the young woman's mangled toes. Thoughts turn to Chris, knowing she can't leave without him. "Have you seen my husband? Do you know what they've done with him?"

Melody begins working the knife faster and harder, forcing more stifled cries from Judy. The sight of the small tear in the tape spurs Melody on; her stomach, though, continues to twist with guilt and nausea. "I heard a noise," she says. "Under the stairs. There's a shelving unit there that wasn't before."

"The old man," Judy cries, 'he said something before about being trapped under the stairs. That must be where they are. Hurry, Melody. Hurry."

And finally, letting out a groan through clenched teeth, Melody manages to work through a strand of the tape. She pulls and unravels it, alternating her glance between Judy's reddened wrists and the concrete steps. Judy offers a relieved sigh, bending her wrists this way and that, new-found hope coursing through her. They're going to get Chris and get the hell out of this place.

Applying the same method as before: twisting, grunting, and pulling like fuck, Melody begins working at the ankles. And as if the legs were the last to be tied, whichever of the loons upstairs becoming lazy with their work, the tape quickly pulls away with little need for the knife. "Let's get out of here," Melody says, helping Judy down from the wooden platform, their embrace instinctive but brief. "Can you walk?"

"Yes, I think so," Judy says, nursing her side as she limps her way to the steps.

Melody watches the lady hobbling away from the orange glow, contemplating the right thing to do. "Judy."

The older lady turns and frowns, looking to Melody as though she's aged twenty years. "Yes?"

She's never really spent much time on it before, but the seriousness of the moment demands it. "Judy, I—"

"What is it, Melody?"

Melody snaps her head towards the wooden pegboard and reaches for the hammer. "You might need a weapon." She joins Judy at the bottom of the stairs, placing the tool into the retiree's hand as though they were Vikings going into war.

"I'm not sure I'll be able to use it," Judy says, following Melody up the steps.

Wrapping her fingers around the cold door handle, Melody turns, deep lines working their way across her forehead and carving into her youth. "Judy, they've already taken a part of you. Don't let them have the rest."

"I'm scared."

"I'm fucking terrified," Melody replies, her heart thundering. "On three we go." She swallows hard, knowing the poor woman would be manic, inconsolable if she knew what was happening to her husband upstairs. *The likelihood is he's already dead.*

"Wait," Judy says, tightening her grip on the handle and performing a couple of practice swings.

Fucking hell, Melody thinks, witnessing the feeble effort. *We've got no chance.* She takes a couple of deep breaths, trying to lower her heart rate. "On three," she says again, praying for a last-second miracle.

Three.

Two.

One.

Judy's scream is instinctive as the door opens, but at the sight of Marge's face, lips offering a wide gummy smile, a little bit of Chris at the edge of them, Melody fails to even lift the knife before the very portable cooking stove catches her square on the nose. In a tangled heap, she and Judy tumble to the hard ground, offering a series of pained grunts and moans.

"You simply must stay for dinner," Marge sings.

As Melody tries to unravel and push herself up, she hears the descending footsteps and the faint tick-tock of the grandfather clock. She pushes her feet against the ground, desperate to move into a less vulnerable position, but before she even gets to her elbows, she feels a sharpness in her neck. "Pretty eyes," she hears Albert say from above. "But you're no longer my favourite; you're a naughty birdie, trying to spoil all little old Alby's fun."

Futilely, needle jutting from her neck, Melody writhes against the cold ground, contemplating her last moments alive will be spent in the basement of a poxy bed and breakfast. Not very rock n' roll, Richie would say. *Definitely not very metal.* She makes brief eye contact with Judy, the guilt of deceit adding to her heaviness. No small talk this time, no foreplay; the tidal wave of blackness is on her quickly.

—7—

Dinner Guest

Part One:
Having Guests for Dinner

Judy tries to open her eyes, her head pounding and the room spinning as though she's halfway through a bottle of vodka. *What the hell?* "Melody?" Her blurred vision offers only Marge and Alby's glistening gums and what look like lopsided pink party hats.

No. God, please, no.

Above the throbbing in her side, she feels a dullish pain in her neck, all hope fading as events come flooding back. Swimming in front of her, Marge's lips move relentlessly but offer only an incoherent drawl. She tries to move, offering a pained groan as she realises she's once again bound.

Christ, will this nightmare ever end?

"Have some, dear," she hears Marge say, the old bag's voice only now slightly distorted. "It's really quite good, especially this part. I've never usually been one for tripe, but this is something else."

Judy blinks several times, shaking her head as if trying to disperse the fog. She looks away from the wavering images of the two old people, their cheeks crammed full, turning her eyes to the rest of the table. Complete with glasses, silverware, and the forever sickening pink tablecloth, Margaret and Albert are putting on a banquet, plates full of meat, goblets of red, and a shit load of taters *and veg.*

"Tender and juicy," she hears Margaret say. "Just how I like it."

And with a crash of subsequent thunder, Judy's back. Back in Hell, in full high definition and crystal-clear sound.

Chris is at the table, staring at the ceiling, arms gone just below the shoulders and his legs nothing but stubs. He's little more than a torso and a head, but his torso ripped open like the frogs she used to dissect in high school science class. Mostly empty, the contents already removed, his stomach resembles an empty tunnel, a ribbed archway with a spine road traversing it. Seated beside him is Melody, head slumped back, a mixture of blood, mucus, and mascara smeared down her cheeks. Judy's unsure if the poor girl is breathing. Noting the plates full of what she guesses to be her husband's glistening innards, the scene finally hits her like a portable stove across the nose, prompting her to turn and vomit towards the floor. *This can't be real. Can't be!* Thunder crackles above as she continues her retching, but something else, too, almost a dull echo.

"Pass the pepper, Alby," Marge says.

Please don't let this be real. Please don't let this be real.

But the horrific sweet smell of the half-cooked meat is unmistakable, and no chant will ever change that. She watches Alby guzzling from a silver goblet, revealing a thick red moustache and pink teeth as he finally brings it down. It's her husband's blood; she knows it is. And that's enough to set her off gagging again.

"Well, that's not being a very good dinner guest," Marge says, slurping up a strand of intestine like it's a wide noodle spaghetti. "You weren't complaining at dinner; you couldn't get enough of my pies."

"Tell her, Marge. Tell her!" Alby cries excitedly.

"You want to know which part of Ezekiel you shovelled down your gullet?"

Judy feels the bile rising again, her mind projecting the image of golden crust housing the tender brown meat on her fork. "Sick fucks."

"I told you she's not nice," Alby says, holding Chris' heart steady with a fork and working the serrated knife into it.

"You were right, petal," Marge says. "I'm sorry we have such rude and ungrateful guests, my love. After all the wonderful cooking you did, this is how she acts. On your special day, too." She glares across the table at Judy, a thin strand of meat dangling from her chin. "You really should be ashamed."

Judy begins to quake like an erupting volcano. *Chris. My Chris.* Unable to hold any longer, the tears flow, raw and unfiltered, her entire life flashing before her eyes. *Everything we planned.*

"Shh. You're too loud," Alby says. "You're ruining dinner."

"You're as bad as she is," Marge yells, slamming one hand on the table and aiming a fork at Melody with the other. "She woke up before you, but as soon as my dear old Alby started taking more of her toes, she screamed like a banshee and passed right on out. Drama queens, for heaven's sake."

"More of her toes," Judy repeats in a trance-like whisper. She looks across at Albert to find him holding a stick full of blackened meat. His tongue snakes out to explore the small tower of flesh before he tilts it into his mouth and sucks the first toe right off the stick.

Judy thinks she's going to be sick again. Arms still bound at her sides, she squirms and grimaces, doing her best to hold it in.

They're fucking mad, and we're all gonna die.

She jolts as more thunder explodes, subsequent lightning basking the horrors spread across the table. Almost immediately she hears that dampened echo again. *No, not an echo. And coming from the other room.*

Thoughts turn to survival.

I'm so sorry, my love.

But Chris is gone, and she's still breathing.

Doing her best not to break down completely, Judy conjures the balcony of their favourite hotel: she and Chris overlooking the streets, soaking up the music of Paris and sipping on a glass of expensive champagne. Marge and Alby's voices fade, but the thunder doesn't, and each time it strikes, she follows with a cacophonous dry retch, trying to disguise that subsequent *noise,* that little glimmer of hope.

Part Two:

Fashionably Late

In time with the explosion of thunder that accompanies the raging storm, Richie grits his teeth and kicks at the weakened wall as hard as he can. He's seen *Shawshank Redemption* a thousand times and hopes to watch it a thousand more if he gets out of this godforsaken place. Dust and plaster sprinkle around him, and he stifles a choke, his head spinning and his ears ringing as they do on the occasions that he forgets his earplugs at a show.

Off balance and disoriented, squinting into the light trickling through the hole, Richie somehow manages to get to his feet. His left arm hangs awkwardly at his side, and every muscle screams in protest. Yet even through his pain and fear, he can't deny the celebratory guitar chords playing in his head. He quietly coughs into his one cooperative hand, staring at the hole in front of him as *the* dust finally begins to settle.

I just went right through the fucking wall. What's more metal than that?

Drawing on his childhood trauma had finally helped him for once, his time spent punching, kicking, and throwing himself against the confines of his youth. Now he's through, and he can hardly believe it.

Alright Richie boy. What now?

But the twinge in his knuckle draws his attention to his right hand: swollen, purplish-green, skin frayed, and bleeding in several places. Relief fades at thoughts of never playing the guitar again, and there's an instinctive urge to scream, to let out all his rage. Still, he manages to hold it in, intending to bring all hell down on this shitty little bed and breakfast.

"Christ on a mother-fucking bike," he mouths, noticing Zeke's severed head staring up at him from the surrounding rubble. Eyes wide behind the cracked lenses of broken glasses, poor Zeke's mouth hangs open in a permanent scream. Adjacent to the spectacled head is a mutilated hand, curled fingers reaching up towards him as though the dead man still pleads for help.

The fire of anger burning hot inside him, Richie steps out from the hole, glancing across at the metal piece of furniture still blocking the door. Muted voices emerge from the kitchen diner, the last place he remembers being before waking up in the crawlspace.

"Fuck this," he mutters. "No more Mister nice guy."

And with his good hand, Richie reaches over, wrapping his fingers around Zeke's lower teeth, and grasping the open jaw. He lifts Zeke's head in his hands like a bowling ball, removing the glasses and performing a few practice swings. Finally satisfied, he marches towards the murmuring voices ready to bowl the match of his life and feeling like an extra from *Dawn of the Dead*, his left leg dragging behind and his left arm swinging redundantly.

Part Three:
Strike

Judy's the first to turn to see Richie entering the room, a manic expression across his face as he swings something over his shoulder. It looks like a head. But it can't be a head.

The makeshift weapon catches Alby on the back of the skull, jolting him forward, the toe kebab jamming into his mouth and forcing a gag. Instinctively, Marge lunges with her fork, but Richie swings a backhand, sending her head snapping to the side, momentum sending her chair over and the apron riding up, revealing knickers the size of a small parachute.

It just can't be. Can't be a—fucking hell, it is! Richie's carrying a fucking head around with him!

She watches him swing it again, catching Alby on his cheek, the party hat flying off, and a chewed-up bit of gristle shooting from the old man's thin lips. The next blow sends the frail fucker to the floor, dentures spilling out.

As the surreal scene unfolds around her, Judy wonders how she'll ever get over such events, knowing it will take a damn sight more than a debrief and a couple of Paracetamol. In a moment of reflection, it all becomes too much for her, and she feels herself begin to sway from side to side, but as Richie slams the severed head down on Melody's plate, she jolts out of a trance, watching the poor kid begin to work at Melody's ties with bloodied and trembling fingers.

"She doesn't have toes anymore," Judy mumbles.

"Come on, baby. I need you to wake up. We're getting out of here," Richie says, fumbling at the string. "I really need you to get with it, Mel. Please, baby!"

"Toes. They took her—" Judy breaks off, watching thick sausage fingers grab the table's edge, plates gravitating towards them as the tablecloth draws away like the tide.

Richie continues working at the rope, managing to slide his finger under the knot. But just as he begins to work it loose, he lets out a high-pitched cry, feeling something sink into his leg. He looks down to see Alby's toothless smile and the old man's bony fingers coiled around the handle of the steak knife jutting out from his charity shop pants. As the old man tries to wrestle the knife free, Richie grimaces and brings his boot down hard on the fucker's face.

"Albyyyyyyyyyyyy!" Marge cries, hearing the snapping sound. She slowly rises, offering a series of huffs and puffs like the big bad motherfucking wolf.

"Come on, Mel. Wake up!" But even as Richie works the string loose, Melody remains limp in the chair, eyes closed. "Shit, Mel. I need you. I've always needed you."

Judy vomits towards the floor once more.

Eyes wide and pinned to the glistening Butcher knife Marge now has in her hand, Richie begins shaking the love of his life. "Wake up, Mel! Wake up!"

"You hurt my Alby, you little shit," the old lady says, using her other hand to prop herself against the table.

A tug on Richie's arm has him snapping his head towards Mel to see her eyes half-open, a goofy drug-induced smile lining her face. "You're so corny," she says.

"I know. I know, baby. We need to go. Please try to get up."

"Where are we?" she slurs. But on the sight of Marge's approaching gums, she suddenly knows exactly where the fuck she is. "Richie!"

"My poor Alby," Marge bellows, spraying fleshy shrapnel across the table. "He's already dying." She puts another big hand on the table and slakes herself towards her groaning husband. "You the type to beat up a dying man?"

With an arm over Richie's shoulder, Melody offers a cry and tries to stand, but as she slides her legs out from under the puckered tablecloth, a high-pitched scream replaces her whimpers. "I've no toes," she cries. "They took my fucking toes, Richie!"

"Took her toes," Judy mumbles.

Supporting Melody's weight, Richie looks down at his lover's feet. Observing there not to be a single toe left, her feet just stumpy blocks, burnt and cauterised, he brings his good hand to his mouth, wondering how the fuck he's going to get them out of there.

"You're not going to leave me, are you?" Judy says, watching Marge working her way slowly around. "Please tell me you're not going to leave me here."

"My dear, Alby," Marge says, finally reaching her husband's side, her tears splashing down onto his sallow cheeks. She puts his teeth back in and plasters his forehead with kisses, further smearing his blood-spattered face. "What have they done to you?"

"We did good, Marge, though," the old man croaks. "Everything off the list. Didn't we do good?"

As the twisted old lovers perform their own on-land, low-budget, slasher version of Titanic, Richie snatches a steak knife from the table. He considers running at the old woman and driving it into the old bag's neck but has an image of her rising and saying, "That's not a knife, this' a knife," and plunging the much larger blade into his chest. Thinking better of it, he hobbles his way to Judy, Mel offering a series of blood-curdling howls as she clings onto him for dear life. "I'm sorry, babe. I'm so sorry," he says, leaning over and working at Judy's string.

"Thank you, Richie," Judy says. "Thank you!"

"My dear sweet monkey," Marge says. "We'll be together again real soon. I promise."

"Ooh-oh, ah-ah."

The old lady draws her husband in, offering one final kiss on his forehead before dragging the large blade across his throat. She holds him close as he chokes, her tears mixing with the *wine* that spills from his neck like an uncorked barrel. "This was supposed to be special," Marge snaps at them. "His final wishes. A good man, as sweet as they come, and you tainted his final supper."

"Fuck off, you saggy cow," Richie yells, still working at the fraying string.

"He had one wish left, though," Marge says, pushing herself to her feet. "And I intend to give it to him. Do you hear me?"

Richie ignores her, pulling at the now frayed string around Judy's wrists. "She's coming, Richie!" Melody yells into his ear.

"Alby requested your whore's eyes," Marge says, standing, bloody knife in hand. "He likes them; wants to be buried with them stuffed in his mouth."

"Richie!" Melody cries.

Richie turns just in time to get his arm out, the steak knife flying from his grip. Before the old lady can try again, he catches her with an elbow straight in the chops. She staggers back a couple of inches, momentarily stunned, but, knife held over her shoulder and offering a snarl, she lunges again. "You'll pay for this!"

Rich blocks the attack, managing to snap both his hands around the big sweaty wrist, but the woman is strong, especially in beast mode. Helplessly, as he tries to keep the blade away from his eyes, he watches Margaret grab a handful of Melody's hair with her other hand.

"Let go, you crazy bitch," Richie yells. "You can't have her."

Judy watches on, still wrestling with the string. It's fraying, working loose, but she still can't find the strength to break through. Her eyes keep falling across what's left of her husband, the dizzying feeling threatening to take her from the fight.

"Let go of me, you fuck!" Melody screams wildly, trying to yank herself free, her club feet sliding clumsily across the floor as Richie continues wrestling with the knife-wielding tree trunk of an arm.

"Let her go," Richie cries. Feeling his grip slipping, he aims a desperate headbutt at the big lady but, in a mistimed lunge, catches her on the right boob.

"Don't make 'em like they used to, Richie," Marge says. "Not sure why you're putting up all this fight for little miss tiny tits over here."

As the three of them continue their pained dance, Judy finally manages to work the string loose, a million thoughts rushing through her head, including throwing the front door open and making a dash for it. Resignedly, she takes a deep breath and drops to the floor, scrambling on all fours to retrieve the steak knife. *This is for you, Chris.* Offering a garbled war cry, partly to mask the pain in her side, she stands and runs at the old woman, driving the steak knife inch-deep into her back.

I did it, Chris! I got the fucker!

But bravery quickly wanes as she watches Marge's eyes grow wide and hears the animalistic snarl leaving her lips. Before she can even think to duck, Marge releases Melody's hair and drives her thick bony knuckles into Judy's cheek, sending her sprawling to the floor.

"Richie, let's go," Melody cries.

Unable to break free from the vice-like grip, Richie decides on a manoeuvre he would never have imagined himself performing on someone before, especially a woman. He grits his teeth and launches his boot right into Marge's nether regions.

The big woman offers a deep exhale and a look of extreme disapproval as her apron rides up. It's as though there were certain rules to adhere to, and Richie's just overstepped the mark. Amputation, fine; locking people in cupboards with dead people, fine; even dining on entrails, acceptable. But kicking a woman in the chuff? Instant disqualification.

Richie drags Melody's arm around his neck again, watching the old woman staggering backwards, her eyes still protesting foul play. "Go!" he screams at Judy, finally turning towards the door.

Judy steps back, wrapping her fingers around the handle. "It's locked."

"The latch!" Richie screams.

Shit! Shit! Shit. Her fingers trembling, her side and head throbbing, Judy works at the latch and turns the handle. But just as the cool breeze rushes in, she hears a tussle behind and a woman's piercing scream. Heart in mouth, she turns, observing the Butcher knife impossibly deep in Melody's back, Richie still holding onto her, face as white as a sheet. "Melody?" he utters in disbelief. "Melody!"

Not even a scream from the poor girl, just a series of pained and fading wheezes. "Always"—she chokes, blood spilling over her bottom lip—"Love you, Ri—"

"Nooooooo!" Richie cries, taking her weight and her last breath against his neck.

"Richie!" Judy tugs relentlessly at his arm, noting Marge behind, holding a rifle and feeding it with ammunition. "Richie, we've got to go!"

"Melody, come back. Come back." This wasn't supposed to happen; he was supposed to be the hero. They'd get home and write a song about it. He'd have to get Banjo to play the guitar, what with his fucked-up hand, but he could do the vocals as he did in the Nag's Head that time. "Like a rabid hound dog," one fan said of his singing, and he'll take that to the fucking grave. "Melody, please!"

"Richie! We have to go!" Judy screams tugging Richie's arm. "She's got a gun!"

Finally, on sight of the rifle, Richie relents, letting himself be dragged into the clear, Melody slumping to the floor in his wake. "I'm so sorry, my love."

"I'll take good care of her, Richie!" Margaret screams after them, bringing the gun around.

Cold to the bone, pain lighting up their bodies, Judy and Richie stagger into the darkness, thunder crackling around them.

"Nothing we can do for her now," Judy says, still pulling at his arm and squinting into the rain. "We need to survive this, Richie."

He's never felt a loss like it. People come and go; he knows that. It's just life. Some he even wanted gone, like that bitch of a foster mother. But Melody changed him, made him complete, and gave him a reason to keep breathing. A sensation seeker, yes, but not this. This is too much.

"Oh Christ," he utters, realisation hitting home with full force. "Oh Jesus, God. I want to go back and kill her. Let me fucking kill her!"

"We're not them, Richie. We're not them. Besides, the woman's as strong as a fucking ox, and now she's armed."

Behind them, in the comparative warmth and artificial light of Beatrice's Bed and Breakfast, Marge pulls the knife from Melody's back and plunges it into the young woman's left eye socket, working the blade underneath. "They are pretty eyes, aren't they, Alby?" It doesn't take long to pry the first one out, and she pops it into the side of her cheek while working on the other. "I'll keep them warm for you, pet."

"Where are the cars?" Richie says, limping after Judy, the ground's heaviness working against them as everything fucking seems to be.

"The dam, I think," Judy replies. "Tyre tracks lead off that way."

"Fuuuuuck!"

"Oh shit, Richie," Judy says, glancing over her shoulder. "She's coming."

As Richie turns, he sees Marge step out from the doorway, lit up menacingly by the porch light. The crazy bitch is smiling, of course. "Where do you think you're going?" she shouts, holding out two small objects in the palm of her hand and the rifle in the other.

Like the fucking geriatric Terminator, Richie thinks. "We're too open here," he yells. "Head for the trees!"

Marge's laughter echoes through the night, rolling into the crackling thunder. "We see you," the big lady cries. "We're coming for you."

−8−

Big Boss Fight

Judy hasn't run for over twenty years, but it's coming naturally enough, likely helped by the deranged woman yielding a rifle and two eyeballs. "You okay, Richie?" A stupid question, she knows, but she needs to bring some humanity to events; Lord knows she's not fucking okay.

Richie groans, wisps of breath peppering the air ahead with ever-increasing frequency as he follows Judy towards the trees. "What's the plan?"

"Stay alive," Judy replies. The pain in her side properly awakening, she turns to see the ominous silhouette of Marge not far enough away for any level of comfort. The big woman stops, lifts the rifle, and takes aim. Preparing for pain, Judy screws her face up, eyes on the treeline only thirty yards ahead. "Run, Richie!"

"I'm trying," he cries, slaking his left leg behind.

Neither of them hears the first gunshot, crashing thunder stealing the show, subsequent lightning, momentarily basking the relative safety of the forest in monochrome. Swearing she catches sight of what looks to be the roof of a vehicle crudely hidden behind foliage, Judy alters her direction, putting their fate into the hands of God. "This way."

But before Richie can even think about changing course, the second shot catches him in his trailing left leg. He lets out a howl towards the moon before crumpling to the wet ground. "You fucking bitch!"

"Can't beat a good old-fashioned hunt," Marge screams from behind. "Do you remember when we went on that hunt in the Australian bush, Alby? The heads we got that day, huh?"

Judy dashes to his side and crouches, noting the expanding patch of blood on his jeans. "Richie, come on." She hooks her arms under his shoulders, encouraging him to try and stand, but he grits his teeth and rolls to his side, holding his thigh. "We can't let this fucker get us, Richie. For Chris. For Melody." She gives up on his shoulders and begins yanking at his arm as hard as she can, her feet sinking into the soft boggy ground. Not nearly far enough away, she observes Marge making ground, lifting the rifle to her shoulder again.

"Maybe it's time I find out what death feels like," he says weakly. "I've never done it."

"Richie, you will fucking stand up right now!"

He offers a high-pitched yelp, his face twisted in agony as he slowly gets to his feet. "Yes, Ma'am."

With Judy leading again, they continue their even more laboured approach to the woods, an orchestra of heavy breathing and pained moans. Richie feels warmth leaking down his legs, unsure if it's blood or piss, but probably the former, light-headedness washing over him. He still can't believe his Melody is gone. There's not a thing he wouldn't do to have her back; he'd even agree to a child. Hell, even two, three, four, even their own little fucking version of Slipknot.

Another shot explodes around them, Judy noticing bark flying off one of the trees ahead. "Come on, Richie!"

He wants to lie down and grieve for his love, but instead, he keeps his eyes on the back of Judy's head and does his best to march through the pain. Timid as a mouse, he thought, when he first met her, but now she's screaming at him, leading the charge, her little bob riding up and down and some of her stomach missing courtesy of the psychotic chimp wannabe with a taste for flesh. Christ, the poor woman only wanted a quiet night at a guesthouse with her husband, maybe a bit of nookie even. For a three-star Bed and Breakfast, you'd perhaps expect the sausages to be undercooked, but not to be in the sausages.

Thunder crackling around them, Judy squeezes through the barbed wire and ducks under the first branch, eyes still fixed on the area where she thought she saw a car. "Over here." Her feet splash and slide against the mud as she uses the trees for support, instinctively ducking again as more gunfire rings out. She turns, ready to spur Richie on, only for a burst of lightning to reveal his body a few feet behind the dilapidated barbed wire fence, face down in the mud.

"Richiiiiiiiiiiiiiie!"

But he doesn't move.

"Just you and me, Judy," Marge calls out from behind. "The strongest of the bunch."

Judy slowly backs away, arms outstretched as she feels for the bark behind. She alternates her glance between the big lady and Richie, willing him to get up, praying she won't be left to face Marge alone. All that talk from Chris about the tree monster, the one that would still snap him from sleep sometimes. Who would have thought they'd stumble upon a real beast in a cosy little B&B in the country?

"Go," Marge says. "I'll give you a head start." She reaches into the pocket of the apron and slides out the eight-inch Butcher knife. "I've got chopping to do."

Before Marge brings the knife down towards Richie, Judy turns and staggers further into the trees. Limbs screaming, side throbbing, and blood whooshing in her ears, she hobbles for her life, feeling the odds well and truly stacked against her. Her feet land heavy as though the ground is trying to swallow them, and as she swings between the trees, she cannot stop the image of Alby flashing in her head.

Like a monkey, Judy!

Those watery eyes, that goddamn toothy smile. "You monkey's fucking cunt!" she screams into the forest.

Chris would want her to keep fighting, though.

Squinting against the pelting rain, she searches the trees ahead, spying the roof of what looks to be an RV, like a Winnebago or something. No sign of Marge as she glances over her shoulder. *What's the plan, Judy? What's the fucking program? Get to the camper. Then what? Are you expecting keys to be in there? Just to drive your way out of this fucking—*

She goes down quickly, cheek sliding across the ground. Cold to the bone, clothes clinging to her skin, she turns over, nursing her ankle and running her eyes across the skeletal canopy. "Help me, Chris. Please help me." Thunder rattles, trees moan, and Judy knows she's on her own, and this is how it is from hereon in.

She forces herself up, wincing as she tests her ankle.

Where's that damn camper?

Disoriented, feeling like she's on the verge of cracking up, she spins around, searching for it. She knows the RV's a shot in the dark, but it's all she has, a glimmer of hope, something to focus on to stop her thinking about Chris' gouged-out chest, his stubby legs, his—*where's the fucking RV?* There's a scream in her throat, and it's all she can do to keep it in.

"Ready or not, here I come," Marge cries.

Alternating course slightly as lightning shows the RV to her left, Judy begins to hobble away from the voice. She digs in deep, biting at her lip, each movement going against what her body screams at her to do. Even without the aid of lightning, she can see it now: the grimy windows, the dull silver of the rims. She makes out the spare tyre, the jerry can strapped to the side, and the towbar with some rope still attached. Not a Winnebago; it's a Coachman, a minor detail but one that helps her stay grounded in reality. There's only darkness within. "Help," she cries anyway, hoping it might be a couple of young'uns taking their chances.

Gunfire explodes, followed by Marge's grinding laughter. "You've got a fine taste in men, Judy. Just the right sweetness." More wheeze-riddled guffawing fills the forest as Judy arrives at the vehicle and desperately yanks at the handle. She can hardly believe it as it pulls open, but her heart sinks as further inspection shows the vehicle empty of heroes.

"Couldn't do much with his pecker, though," Marge cries. "Alby did make it into a cute little pig in a blanket for me, though, that sweet man."

Shut up. Shut up. Shut up, you mad cow. The RV is clean but unimpressive: wood-panelled interiors, basic cream furnishings, and four lime green cushions strategically placed to break the monotony. 'Retro,' Chris would have called it if those fuckers hadn't already scooped his insides out.

She spies a picture frame next to a transistor radio and an unfinished crossword puzzle on a small pull-out table. *A puzzle*—something so ordinary at the centre of such chaos. And momentarily, she's back in their bedroom, Chris next to her reading his latest spy thriller, a cup of hot cocoa on either side.

What do I do, Chris?

As thunder booms, her side offers a sharp reminder there's a piece of her missing and that she's knee-deep in shit. She reaches over towards the frame and brings it closer, tilting it towards the moon. "You've got to be fucking kidding me." Hoping her eyes must be playing tricks, she brings the frame closer still, but the scream in her throat finally escapes. The picture depicts a younger version of Marge and Albert, one she assumes to be from their time spent in the Amazon, their arms around a couple of tribespeople and all holding spears of some sort.

This can't be. It just can't be.

Everywhere she looks, she sees their faces; abhorrent smiles offering blood-stained teeth and hanging entrails. Panic has her, digging its icy hand within and exploring, tormenting, tapping its fingers up and down her spine, sending her body into a violent frenzy of shaking. She tilts the crossword puzzle towards her, snatching the metal pen as it rolls, running her eyes over some of the answers: chimp, bananas, tyre, monkey, swing, ooh oh, monkey, monkey, monkey, monkey. She rotates the pen between her fingers, noting the word 'Alby' etched across the side. At the front of the cabin, shoved down the side of the driver's seat, she sees half a dozen slightly blackened banana skins. And stuck to the dashboard, as if she needs even more proof, is a head-bobbing monkey, a big smile breaking its cunty little face in two as it clenches a banana with its right hand.

Oh fuck. Oh fuck. Oh—

Keys! If the RV was open, maybe they're—

A gunshot snaps her attention to the window. That was close. Very close. No sign, though. She scans the trees, her eyes nervously flitting back and forth like a cicada trying its luck. *Fuck. Where is she?*

Judy slides the pen into her back pocket and leans over, checking in the ignition, but nothing. A moment of excitement washes over her as she flips the vanity mirror, but as seems to be the day's trend, the action only ends in soul-destroying disappointment. *Movies are full of shit.*

Attention on the rear of the RV again, her eyes search the kitchen area, noting the fire blanket and small extinguisher hanging from the wall. She moves to the sets of drawers beneath the small round sink and opens the first, expecting to find cutlery and perhaps a tin opener. But what awaits pushes the last of her sanity off the plank.

She grabs the first transparent bag, lifting it to the moonlight, running her eyes over the locks of hair and yellowing human teeth. The slightly larger bag beneath looks to Judy like an assortment of dried fruit, but she knows the truth will be much more sinister. At the back of the drawer is a bag full of driver's licenses, passports, college cards, and some photographs she can't bring herself to view. And even further back, she finds a retainer and a perfectly preserved toe coated in a transparent glaze.

Little keepsakes to remind us of the people we met.

"Souvenirs," she says, dropping the bag and closing the drawer. She opens the second, hoping for something different, perhaps even a weapon, something to give her a fighting chance, but all she finds is a collection of newspaper articles. Each editorial seems to be written in a different language, depicting pictures of houses, alleys, and even a beach, none of which helps. Halfway through the pile, though, she recognises the French word *meurtre.* "Murder."

She opens the third drawer to reveal two rolls of tape, various lengths of string, a gas fire lighter, and umpteen halfway burned candles. "Jesus wept." Hardly able to comprehend the gall of her husband's killers, driving around England with an RV full of evidence from goodness knows how many victims, she searches the night, thinking death to be inevitable.

They must have done this a hundred times before. What chance do I have?

One hell of an ordeal that she knows is coming to an end. Anger displaces some of her fear as she contemplates how the old couple has turned her life upside down and ripped her heart out.

Marge will probably do just that, Judy. Sear it, season it, and eat the fucking thing.

The knock at the window jolts her, and she snaps her head towards the glass to see the old bag's squished-up nose, matted hair, and dinner-plate eyes.

"Are you coming out to play, Judy?" Marge says. "There's nowhere left to run. Let's two old gals do this the right way."

Judy searches the room again, desperately looking for something that would at least pass for a half-decent weapon. A thunder strike fails to disguise the pounding blood in her ears and the small, garbled cry that leaves her lips.

"Moody Judy, chicken on Tuesday." The old lady bangs on the window once more, this time using the butt of the gun. "I'm going to leave the gun at the door, Judy, and stand next to the big oak."

Judy studies Marge's face, trying to delve beyond the insanity. *Maybe she wants out now that dear old Alby's worm food? Maybe being put to death is on her fucking bucket list.*

"No tricks, Judy," Marge says, disappearing from view but hitting the gun against the side of the RV to let Judy know where she is. "This is your chance for revenge, to kill me if you've got the stones."

Getting to her weary feet, Judy grimaces and snatches the fire extinguisher from the wall. Her fingers tighten around its neck as she tracks the tapping all the way around to the door. She holds her breath, realising she should be there, blocking the door, stopping Marge from just tugging it open and putting a bullet in her head.

But the tapping stops. And she hears Marge's wheezes fading into the distance.

"Don't knock it 'til you try it, Judy. Murder, I mean. It's like getting your cherry popped every time, and at our age, that's a feeling long since passed, ain't it?"

Judy releases the extinguisher and puts her face to the window, continually wiping at her breath cloud as she watches Margaret's quick shuffle towards the large oak tree. *Shit. Fuck. Shit. Fuck. Fuck. Shit. Fuck. Shit.*

"I'm ready, Judy," Marge says, her World's Best Grandma blood-soaked apron kicking up in the wind as she turns.

Taking deep breaths doesn't help; her fear back and turned up a notch. She considers pushing open the door and making a run for it, but there's no mistaking the stickiness that continues to leak down her side. There's a suspicion she can only stand up because adrenaline keeps her going— survival instinct, love it or hate it.

"Better hurry before I change my mind, Judy. Ain't good for my complexion with all this rain."

Inhale. Exhale. Inhale.

Finally, Judy grabs the handle and pushes the door open to reveal the rifle. *Inhale. Exhale.* Half-expecting Marge to appear from nowhere and charge her down, she snaps it up, not feeling any safer. Pointing the rifle ahead, she follows the RV around until she finally sees Margaret patiently waiting, smiling through the rain.

"Come as close as you like, dear; I promise not to bite."

"Forgive me if I don't believe that."

Margaret's smile deepens. "Look at it this way, though, Judy. It's been one hell of an experience, don't you agree? Yes, you could have had a hot chocolate before bed, discussed the following day's weather with hubby and even got up to a continental breakfast. But what's memorable about that? How would that ever get the juices flowing like the entertainment I've provided. You're hurt and bleeding, but I bet this is the most alive you've probably ever been."

Judy lifts the rifle, trying to control her fear and rage. She edges forward, working on her breathing, the sight of the gun wavering frantically.

"Aren't you going to say thank you?"

"I drink cocoa, bitch. There's a big fucking difference!"

"Ah, Judy. Anger isn't our friend; anger is a strong emotion that can overwhelm us. Killing requires a calm heart. You must embrace the power, allow it to wash over you."

Perhaps less than ten feet between them, Judy stops, the rifle suddenly feeling impossibly heavy in her hands and the rain harder and colder. She eyes Marge through the sight, who maintains her hunched-over stance, and butter wouldn't melt smile. If it weren't for the blood-splattered apron, the maniacal look behind her eyes, and the fact that entrails were dangling from the corner of her mouth only moments ago, the old bag could pass for being human.

"Judge Judy and executioner," Margaret announces, as though she's been waiting hours to say it.

"Just shut up, will you? For one goddamn minute, shut the fuck up." Judy curls a finger around the trigger, screwing her eyes shut, desperately trying to steady the rifle.

"I'm ready, Judy. Let's do this."

Judy suddenly feels so weak, the wind almost taking her off her feet. The harder she clutches the gun, the more the sight wavers.

"You can't do it, can you?"

Thunder explodes directly above, but Judy keeps her full attention and aim on Margaret. Her left leg buckles, but she stays standing. Visions of the dinner table flash in her mind, the plates full of—

"Meat. That's all we are, Judy. Just walking, talking, slabs of meat, and being any better than anyone else depends only on how we're cooked."

"I told you to shut up." Fingers on the trigger, Judy screws her eyes almost closed.

"I'm just trying to make it easy for you," Marge continues. "Just animals with dignity."

Judy's life with Chris flashes before her, leading to recent evenings discussing future plans. It feels like a chunk of her has been taken away, not just from her side. And this fucker in front of her is responsible.

"Although saying that, your Chris did squeal like a pig at the end. Squeeeeeee. Squeeeeeeee." The old lady begins to laugh, which quickly becomes a coughing fit.

"Fuck you, Marge," Judy says, squeezing down on the trigger, her heart skipping.

Nothing but a click.

Thunder rolls across, once again adding demonic bass to Marge's raspiness. "You silly dumb fuck, Judy," the old lady says, taking a step forward. "What an anti-climax to the evening that would have been."

Judy begins her retreat, wielding the rifle like a baseball bat. Once again, there's a temptation to take off, but she's in no man's land here, and besides, she's not sure how far she'd get. She looks down at her shirt to see the blood spreading once again.

"Last thing on my bucket list is a fight to the death, Judy." Margaret takes another few steps before crouching down and picking up a large branch. "We saw it in the jungle from time to time, an honourable display some might consider simple savagery. But what a way to go, eh? Better than dying in your sleep or from eating too many hamburgers, don't you agree, Judy?"

Last thing on my bucket list is a fight to the death. No, Judy doesn't agree. She can't remember too many of them at the moment due to a slightly heightened level of anxiety, but some of theirs included holding hands on a gondola in Venice, riding a camel in Egypt, and hot-air ballooning in

New Zealand. Nowhere on their list did it mention a fight to the death.

Judy continues her retreat, weaving between the trees, thoughts turning to the fire extinguisher in the campervan. *Maybe I can blind the old bag.* Deciding it would give her a much-needed advantage, she readies herself to run, psyching herself up for the impending fire bolts.

"You have youth on your side, dear." Margaret whips the branch down into the palm of her hand. "A silly old codger like me should be child's play."

But they both know that's not true. Judy's already seen how strong Marge is and only has to look at her arms, almost indistinguishable from some of the surrounding tree trunks, to know one swipe could send her directly to sleepy town.

Three.

Two.

One.

Judy jumps out, hurling the empty rifle at Marge, who recoils to avoid the blow. Cutting her losses, she takes her chances and makes her way towards the van.

"Oh, I like it better when they run," Marge says, coming back around the tree and kicking the gun into the darkness.

Exhausted, praying for it all to end, Judy swings herself into the RV and reaches for the fire extinguisher. She imagines Marge coming up behind her, the thought sending her heart thumping and blood pounding in her ears. She can't think. Can't breathe. She needs ideas. Ideas are good. Ideas keep people breathing. But still, the best she can come up with is to spray the old bag with the fire extinguisher and then bring the fucking thing across her head.

Okay.

Surprised by how light it feels, she grips the extinguisher firmly in her right hand and pulls herself from the vulnerability of the RV door. She turns, ready to face her nemesis, holding her ground as Marge approaches.

"I hope you put up a bit of a fight. Some just cave, telling me to make it quick. For those, I usually take my sweeeeeet time."

Thunder roars above.

Six feet away, Marge pauses.

Judy takes a deep breath, eyeing the woman who appears even wider than before, rounded shoulders like a pro-fucking-wrestler heaving up and down.

And as the lighting finally flickers, Marge makes her move, wielding the branch above her shoulder and issuing a blood-curdling cry. She swings, but Judy ducks, the branch skimming off the top of her hairdo, the one she paid nearly two hundred for only last Wednesday.

"You bitch," Judy cries. Gritting her teeth, she pulls the pin and presses the handle, pointing the extinguisher towards Marge's face.

Nothing.

Will you give me a fucking break? She releases and squeezes down again, but still nothing. "Motherfucker!"

Marge leans her head back and laughs. "That's been empty for a year, my dear. I've been meaning to refill it, but my old brain never can remember."

And as though a match to a flame, Judy suddenly feels the fire of anger raging through her. She offers a high-pitched war cry, wielding the empty extinguisher in her right hand as she charges towards the battle axe in the apron. Marge turns, readying the branch, suddenly aware of her stationary vulnerability.

Both swing simultaneously, and both connect, the branch whipping against Judy's arm and the extinguisher catching Marge on the side of her neck. They lunge for each other, tying themselves up, unable to get strikes in as they dance under the moonlight.

"Cried like a girl, your Chris. Begged like a dog."

"He was a better man than your chimp sidekick could ever be."

Marge spins them both around, forcing Judy's back into a tree. "Alby was a fucking legend. Should have seen him back in the day." Spittle spraying into the night, they continue their brawl, holding each other at bay, but Marge just getting the better of it.

"A goddamn loon with googly eyes," Judy says through gritted teeth, muscles tearing in her arm as it descends to the side.

The big woman letting out a wild roar and breaking free from Judy's grip. Judy cowers as the branch comes down, the makeshift weapon striking her on the back, prompting a yelp. She tries to stagger away, but Marge won't let go, the empty extinguisher redundantly dancing between them.

"To the death," Marge cries, bringing the branch behind her shoulder again.

"Yours!" Judy yells, screwing her face up and aiming a knee between Marge's legs.

Both let out a wild groan, the branch greeting Judy's cheekbone but the knee a direct hit, releasing Judy from Marge's grip.

"WHY DO PEOPLE KEEP KICKING ME IN THE—"

Crashing thunder steals Marge's last word as though they are the very centre of the storm. Taking her chance, Judy hobbles the best she can into the trees, feet slipping and splashing through the ever-deepening puddles as she ducks under branches, looking for a place to hide. Finally, she leans back against the widest trunk she can find, nursing the extinguisher and catching her breath.

"Oh, Judy. What a day," Marge says, following with a cacophonous coughing fit.

Shut up, you old bag. Shut up. Shut up. Shut up. Poking her head out from the bark, Judy watches Marge side-on. The burly woman's wearing a big old smile and has her hands out, branch-free, catching the rain as if enjoying every second of this nightmare. It reminds Judy of the brief time she spent doing amateur dramatics and that one woman called Sheila who thought her farts smelled like roses. Taco Tuesday put an end to that.

"This was how it was meant to be, Judy. The storm brought you to the door, to me. Come out now, dear, and let fate take its course."

Judy watches Marge twenty feet west before swinging around the bark, creeping as stealthily as her oozing side and stinging back will allow. As thunder rolls above, she sticks to the trunk of one of the smaller trees until the subsequent lightning has had its fun.

"Come on, Judy. Come out and fight. I don't even have a weapon."

But Judy has little fight left. She rests against the back of the RV, trying to conjure a survival plan. Something. Anything. She runs her eyes over the jerry can, thinking she could somehow pour it over the old woman and use the firelighter. *It's pissing down with rain, you idiot. And besides, this isn't one of those violent Quentin Tarantino movies that Chris used to watch.* Although, the more she comes to think of it—

"Thought you had more than this, Judy. Bet you've been hiding all your life. The stick up your ass is why your husband craved adventure so much, isn't it? You're the real reason he's dead. It's your fault, Judy."

"I'm coming out," Judy finally croaks, her whole life flashing before her. "I can't do this." She pushes from the RV and walks defeatedly towards the small clearing, her body, a shivering, damp mess.

Marge turns and begins looping back, her hands falling to her side and the smile fading. "No! You have to fight. This is how it ends. A fight to the death!"

"I'm not fighting you, Marge. I'm not like you."

"But it's the last thing on my list," she says, her tone that of a child not being allowed ice cream.

"Maybe you'll just have to let me go then."

"That? That was your plan, Judy?" Marge offers her infamous raspy laugh. "We both know that's not going to happen."

Thunder explodes, lightning basking the stage for the final scene.

"Well then, do what you will."

Less than ten feet between them, Judy's instinct is to run as far away from this devil personified as her body will take her. She stands her ground, though, tossing the extinguisher on the ground and putting her hands behind her back.

"I'm disappointed in you, Judy," Marge says, stopping just a couple of feet in front of her. "That time before, I saw fire in your eyes. Probably the only time you've ever really felt anything in your sad little life."

"Just stop talking, you silly old fuck. Do what you need to do."

"They never really came close to catching us." Marge rests her left hand on Judy's shoulder as if sharing a special moment. "No motive, see. No specific profile. Wasn't like we did it in anger or felt compelled like the ones claiming to hear the voices. Those people meant as much to us as pieces in a board game."

"Will you stop fucking talking?"

Marge nods, rain splashing from her chin and nose. "I do like you, Judy. For that reason, I'll make it quick." She wraps her big hands around Judy's throat and begins to squeeze.

Pressure already unbearable, things in her neck cracking and popping, Judy coils her fingers around the metal pen. She draws it from her pocket and, in one fluid and valorous moment that even surprises her, brings the nib deep into Marge's throat. The old woman's eyes widen, but her grip somehow tightens. Thunder rattles again, disguising some of Marge's choking sounds but not the stream of blood working across the ripples of her saggy flesh.

"I'll kill you," the old woman wheezes.

"You already have," Judy rasps, feeling her eyes beginning to bulge. She snatches back the pen, this time driving it into the side of the old lady's throat. And again. And again. And again. Finally, the pressure around Judy's neck relents, Margaret slumping to the ground with her big hands to her throat, emitting a series of gargled chokes. "I'm coming, Alby," she manages to croak, her big legs slapping wildly against the mud.

Sucking in the icy air, Judy drops to her knees with the pen raised. She looks into Marge's eyes, a pang of inexplicable guilt washing over her, the woman now looking nothing more than a helpless old fogie with a dozen holes in her neck. Life visibly leaving her eyes, and only a dampened and incoherent whispering emerging from her lips, the old woman drops her arms to her side.

Thunder rumbles, subsequent lighting falling across Marge's face and emphasising the magnificent red streaks decorating her neck.

Just do it, Judy. Do it! Why is she hesitating, she wonders? After all that the woman has put her through. *I'm not like her. I'm not like her.*

More raspy whispers emerge from Marge, her eyes widening further as if what she's saying has to be heard. Hovering the pen above Marge's head, ready to strike, Judy leans over. She brings her ear a few inches from Marge's lips, finally hearing the woman's dying words: "Thank you."

What feels only like a sting, Judy puts down to her wound opening further. But the flicker of a smile across Marge's mouth has her looking down, observing blood spilling down the wrong side of her shirt. "You fucker." She drops the pen and puts a hand to her side, tracing her fingers across the handle of the butcher knife. *Not fair; I won.* But with a garbled scream, she crumples to the ground next to Marge, joining in with the orchestral death cries.

Offering pained wheezes, Marge searches through the dirt with her fingers, weakly grasping at the pen on contact and tracing the letters of her beloved's name. They'll be together again soon; she just knows it. Her other hand works like a crawling spider back into the pocket of her World's Greatest Grandma *apron,* wrapping around the two soft orbs. *Can't forget those.*

Side by side, the two ladies spend their last twitching seconds staring at the moon through the naked canopy of trees. Judy thinks about her family, of the things she and Chris will never get to do, their bucket lists unfinished by a long shot. She thinks about many things as she smooths and turns her wedding ring, but also about what Margaret said, *Better than dying in your sleep.*

"Rock n roll, Richie," she manages to say on approach of the black tide.

I got her for you, Chris. I got—

Beatrice

Only her faith in the good Lord has kept Beatrice going, chilled to the bone, scarred beyond recognition, and pain lighting her up everywhere. She doesn't know how long she spent meandering through the woods, sometimes passing out from the pain, only for the merciless cold rain to bring her back to consciousness. Dress in tatters, some of it attached to her skin and not just from the rain, she finally stumbles from between the last of the trees and stretches her blistered arms towards the dirty yellow light of the petrol station.

Praise be. Praise be to God.

Through the glass and her one untarnished eye, she spots young Jake Talbot behind the counter, phone up to his face. Beatrice knows his mother, bit of a 'legs-open all hours' sort, not one of God's children, but she can't afford to be overly picky right now. Gritting her teeth, she wraps a sizzled palm around the handle, and, using the last of her strength, yanks the door open.

The Lord is my strength and my shield.

At the bell's tinkle, Jakes punches in the last few letters of the text and hits send. Usually, he would greet customers with small talk about the weather, possibly some cheesy one-liners. "Nice weather for ducks," he'd said to his last customer, but that was over an hour ago, the storm rightly keeping ordinary folks inside. As his eyes fall across the crinkle-cut geriatric who makes her way towards him, words fail him for the first time. "Phone. I need to use your phone, please," the woman croaks, her words loaded with pain.

He should have known it was too good to be true; a quiet shift and as much cherry Slurpee as he could drink. He'd asked Tony if he could finish early, what with lack of trade, but Tony, being the greedy sort, all but laughed at him. Now he's got a zombie in his shop asking to use his phone. "What—what happened?" he says, handing over his most precious belonging.

"No, you need to dial." Beatrice lets her weight fall against the counter. "My fingers—" The tears come without warning, the rest of her words an incoherent garble. Flashbacks to the night fill her head, and she knows she'll take the faces of those Devil's disciples to her grave.

Cursing his bad luck, Jake makes his way around to the old lady. She reminds him of when his dad leaves the meat on the grill too long, all charred and leathery, fit only for the birds. "It's going to be okay," he says. But he's not so sure, the poor old bag looking like an extra from World War Z. Close-up, her face looks even worse, a knotted and puckered patchwork of reds and pinks. He feels helpless, out of his league, the one-hour induction session when he started the job, not extending to dealing with crispy old ladies.

"I'm not feel—" As Beatrice's legs finally fail her, and she begins sliding down the counter, Jakes takes her hand, wincing at the feel of her damp skin. He cringes as some flakes off at his touch and sprinkles to the floor like cigarette ash. Noticing her violent tremble, he quickly shrugs off his jacket and carefully wraps it around the old woman's shoulders so as not to hurt her and cause more skin to fall. "Who do you want me to call?" *An ambulance or a priest?"*

"I don't know." It's the first time she's stopped to take in the damage. She runs her fingers across an arm, up her chest, and face, knowing none of her expensive creams will be able to fix this. She thinks about her son, hoping it's not too late. "Perhaps the police first. Yes, the police."

Jake tries to stay as calm as possible as he taps the keys. He holds the phone to the poor old lady's cooked ear and nods, wondering how on earth she's still alive. "It's ringing."

The old lady takes a deep breath and bites at her savaged lip.

Thunder rolls above, but the worst of it is over, even the rain notably pelting the glass with a little less vigour. As the old lady begins her tale of horror, Jake slides down the counter next to her, thinking no person should ever have to endure such an ordeal. The words come out fast, frantic, almost running into each other, and it's all Jake can do not to cry.

"—in the barn. Laughing and throwing liquor at me. Marge was the worst; I could see the Devil in her eyes. Told me that they had my son, Ezekiel, that they were thinking about eating him, my boy, my wonderful boy."

Jake's skin tightens around his skull. He lets out a little shudder, feeling slightly less safe than he did five minutes ago. He searches the night beyond the glass, half-expecting to see more walking dead approaching the petrol station looking for a midnight snack.

"Told me I was too old to eat, that my skin would be tough like a pair of old boots. Flicked the match at my dress and left me for dead. God is good, though, and brought the rain before the flames brought death. I know in my heart that my

Ezekiel is still alive, too, God willing. Please come quickly."

Jake watches the old woman's burnt hand fall to her side, still clutching his phone. *I don't think I want that back.*

"Thanks, Jake," she rasps.

He wonders how the old woman knows his name but guesses it's likely through his mother. His mother knows a lot of people, or at least they all know her.

"I'll pray," he says.

Sirens scream in the distance.

And for the first time ever, Jake does. He prays to all Hell and back that they'll soon hear sirens, that the crispy old lady won't die with his precious phone held between her Kentucky-fried fingers.

ABOUT THE AUTHORS

Mark Towse is an Englishman living in Australia. He would sell his soul to the devil or anyone buying if it meant he could write full-time. Alas, he left it very late to begin this journey, penning his first story since primary school at the ripe old age of 45. Since then, he's been regularly published in  anthologies and magazines and, to date, has six novellas to his name, including *Nana*, *Crows*, and *Hope Wharf*.

Chisto Healy has over 200 published stories out in the wild for you to find. He is the author of the *Sunnycrest Apartment* series starting with *Accidental Murderer in Apt 34* and the *Women of Avaron* series that starts with the *Guardian trilogy*. He is regularly featured on the  YouTube show Fear from the Heartland that airs on Wednesdays and has over 30 creepypastas you can listen to. You can find him on Facebook, Twitter, Instagram, TikTok, or www.chistohealy.com He lives in North Carolina with his fiancee, her very cool mom, three amazingly talented children that he is endlessly proud of, a very clingy dog, and an absurd amount of cats. He loves them all.

OTHER NOVELS FROM
THE EVIL COOKIE PUBLISHING

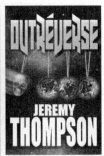

ANTHOLOGIES FROM
THE EVIL COOKIE PUBLISHING

WWW.THEEVILCOOKIE.COM

Printed in Great Britain
by Amazon

16587658R00102